BLIND EYE

KRIS LEITH

Paperback: 978-1-959224-98-3
eBook: 978-1-959224-99-0
Library of Congress Control Number: 2023908837

Ordering Information:

Prime Seven Media
518 Landmann St.
Tomah City, WI 54660

Printed in the United States of America

*This book is for those who dare to be different
and do things their own way.*

ACKNOWLEDGEMENTS

This is for family and friends who inspired me to change direction and try something different.

Chapter 1

The explosion knocks me to the floor. Wood splinters and chunks of drywall land on me, filling my lungs with choking dust. This isn't what I have planned. Everything has turned to shit in a matter of seconds.

"You'll never get her back, Emery!" a voice yells from the other end of the house.

I lift my head slowly, lights flickering on and off randomly. The back of my head feels as if it's on fire. I reach back slowly to touch it and feel something warm and sticky.

"Fuck," I mumble.

"Wrong place, wrong time yet again, Emery!"

Lifting myself up onto my hands and knees, my head swims with darkness, and I instantly feel dizzy. My head throbs violently as I search the chaos on the floor for my gun. The lights flick off again, and I fall into darkness. All I can hear is my breathing. Then another noise comes through the night: the sound of sirens screaming.

"God damn it." My hand knocks against something metal, and I grope for it.

"Here comes the cavalry, Emery, might not be safe here for any of us.!"

The something metal turns out to be my pistol. I pull the slide back and let it slam home again. Thankfully, the suppressor is still attached to the muzzle. That's some comfort—I'd thought for a second that the grenade had ruined my chances. The lights begin to flicker again, and I can see more clearly; the dust has settled somewhat. I rise to my feet and look into what's left of the mirror hanging on the wall over the sink. In the sputtering, I can see my face is covered in blood and plaster, looking like something out of a horror movie. No time for vanity now. I push the pistol out in front of me and move slowly towards the door. I can't lose her, mustn't lose her. If I don't get her back, I know she will die.

"What's wrong? You scared of the feds?" I yell back. I hear nothing for a short moment, and then I hear it again. The laughter. That cackle belongs to the jerk-off that has been taunting the police, and me, for several months. His type of cat-and-mouse games means innocent people are getting caught in the cross fire.

"Don't worry, Emery, I'll take extra good care of her! Extra special care!" I could almost see the grin on his face as he said it, making my skin crawl. I had seen enough of what this mutt's idea of "special care" was, and what he had done to the girls he'd kidnapped was far from human.

"Just let her go, it's me you want!" Slowly I eased around the doorframe. Looking down the long hallway towards the voice, there is no immediate indication of where he's hiding. The lights flick off again, and I hear a muffled cry.

"No, Emery, that's not how the game is played. You know that."

My vision blurs momentarily then swims back into focus. Looking the other direction down the hallway, I can see lights approaching fast.

"Time for us to leave, Emery. Sorry I can't stay for the reunion, but y'know, you have my best wishes." The voice stated in a taunting tone. This mutt really thinks he has everyone under control.

I hear a window smash from a room or two away, followed by another muffled scream. The next sound was something that I had heard before and immediately made my blood run cold. Something hit the instep of my boot, something hard. I only had a split second to react. I leap for an open doorway and slam it shut as I roll through it.

The explosion blows the door inward, ripping it off its hinges and slamming it against the far wall of the bedroom. A slightly different course could have been bad news for me, but thankfully, most of the blast has been absorbed by the door. I stand up quickly, my ears still ringing from the concussion. The end of the hallway is scattered with light.

"Not good. Definitely not good."

I leave the smoking ruins behind and stumble into the night.

Chapter 2

Eighteen weeks earlier

Dan dropped himself into the seat in front of his computer and moved the mouse. The screen redrew into his home page and he clicked through to his usual search engine time to see whether his favourite vigilante had been up to anything. Dan was sure he was ahead of the cops on this one, and it gave him a peculiar thrill. His *Hideandseek* program had confirmed the patterns he had spotted, a couple of recent murders of undesirables, and the logins of a few usernames on certain Web site message boards. He was pretty sure that some of the usernames were cops out fishing too, but that feeling of being ahead of the game was only confirmed when he reviewed the logs from *Hideandseek*.

He typed in the search bar and looked up a particular Web site. It was still there, amazingly enough. He read the text, not that there was a lot to read, but he read it anyway. There were three buttons. Ignoring the first two, he went straight to the contacts list. All that was listed was a phone number and an e-mail address. He had already sent two e-mails to the address and had received no replies.

He lifted the phone and quietly dialled the number. It rang and rang as it had before. Frustration was about to get the better of him when the phone was answered.

"Hello," the voice said. Nothing superhero or vigilante-sounding about it. Dan wasn't sure why this disappointed him.

Dan paused a beat before beginning to speak. "I'm looking for the caretaker of this phone." Silence filled the line.

"Why?" Despite the question, the voice sounded uninterested. "I believe that we may be able to help each other," Dan replied.

"I'm sorry, you'll have to look elsewhere for assistance," the voice replied.

Dan felt the person on the end of the phone was about to hang up.

"Wait! At least hear what I have to say!" He realised he'd said it a little too loudly and silently cursed himself for not keeping his cool. The line stayed quiet.

"Oriental Parade opposite the Copthorne hotel tomorrow, eight o'clock.

Don't waste my time," the voice finally replied, and the line went dead.

Dan dropped the phone into the cradle and looked at the screen in front of him. He was right, he was sure of it. Either that or he was off to meet a raging psycho. He shut the computer down and went to join his wife in bed.

Chapter 3

I sat in front of the computer looking at a blank screen. I had just dropped the phone on the desk.

"What the hell does this guy want?" I asked the darkness around me. Nothing. Silence. I had no intention of meeting him but .. . but something told me he might be of use. The number was the same as several others on my missed call log, so he'd tried several times to get in touch. The site with my phone and e-mail details wasn't one that the average Joe would stumble across, and he didn't sound like the other types of calls I'd received. Most would never ring twice, let alone four or five. I was sure that this was also the same guy who'd sent a couple of emails, offering his help.

It was going to cost a fortune for me to fly to Wellington at short notice, but I figured if this guy was as serious as he was persistent, then maybe it would be worth my while. I picked up the landline next to the computer and dialled a number for a travel agent.

"One return ticket to Wellington, please. Carry-on only." The bubbly- sounding Lady gave me a flight number and ticket reference. The flight would get me there at three o'clock in the afternoon, but that was fine. I needed to see someone before I went to this impromptu meeting. I hung up the phone and then dialled another number. Answer phone. Damn it—he never answers his phone.

"I'm coming down. Be there just after three." Then I hung up. I opened the Web browser on the screen and typed in an address. It was an address that I used regularly. It led to a bulletin board where people could post comments and chat with each other. A lot of people used it, and a lot of people knew me. Or at least knew my username. The rest was window dressing.

Spangle 36. Instantly I had twelve messages waiting to be read. Three were a redirect from my user account. I'd get to them later. The rest were garbage but worth checking out. One read "Get sex here." Another stated how for a small fee, I could do anything to a sixteen-year-old girl. I sighed; some people will do anything to get laid.

I deleted everything except one that said "toys" and the three from my persistent friend. I opened the message that said "toys," and it led me to a chat room.

Hello Spangle36 what you doin? it asked. I read and reread the question. It could have been some innocent kid hoping to find someone to talk to, or it could be some sick fuck hoping to find someone to rape. Or murder. I don't think it really mattered; the end result would be the same. A life ruined.

Not much. What about you? I typed, and then hit Enter. I was instantly assaulted by another message.

What are you wearing? What does the 36 stand for? It asked. I read the message twice before I replied.

Who's asking?

Someone who is looking for a little love.

I waited, not wanting to be seen as easy in this mutt's eyes. Of course, I could have it all wrong, but I didn't think so.

Well? The next message asked. I continued to wait. Waited to see if he would crack and get abusive or not.

Come on. What's the worst that could happen; I'm just looking for someone to have a little fun with.

I don't think my boyfriend would be very happy with me if he found out that I was talking to someone else, I replied.

Don't worry about him. It would be our little secret.

I read the text again. It looked innocent enough. I looked at his user profile. It said his name was Graff 56. He was male, and that was it. I had seen this kind of user before, and nothing useful came of it.

Ok. I guess it would be all right. I kept it tame as I didn't want to drag it on. But that's not what Graff 56 had in mind.

I'd like to meet tonight, Graff 56 stated.

My fingers danced over the keys, deciding. *Ok where?* I finally replied.

Ihumatio road. Out near the airport. Do you know the one? An online map link appeared.

I looked at the address. I'd been there before. Another victim had been found dumped on the side of the road. She had been raped and mutilated post-mortem.

Ok I'll be there in an hour, and then I killed the link. I had to get moving; it was going to take me at least forty-five minutes to get there. I grabbed my coat and headed for the door.

Chapter 4

Megan picked up the newspaper and flipped it open. She ignored the front page and went to the next. The article of interest had been kept off the front page, at least. It described a police update into the investigation of a body found near the airport. He had been shot twice at close range with a pistol. Once in the forehead and once in the chest. The pistol had been recovered, but no prints had been found on it.

She wasn't surprised at the details that had been released. She had already been to half a dozen crime scenes. All the same. Men had been executed, shot at close range, in the forehead then in the heart. What really tweaked her interest in these cases was that all the victims were then found to be tied into heavy crime of some description. The latest had been some asshole that trolled for girls over the Internet. A search of his home had revealed the extent of his interest. He'd had portable hard drives filled with videos and images using girls as young as six or seven.

As far as she was concerned, he got what he deserved. Consequently, she wasn't about to go looking too hard for whoever pulled the trigger.

She picked up her coffee cup from the countertop as she read the article again. She knew Captain Holmes would be all over this like the proverbial rash, and she also knew that she would be dragged into it sometime in the near future. It was surprising that she'd been able to dance around the edges for this long.

Megan was a psychologist and had been studying the criminal mind during her time on the force. What intrigued her about this vigilante was he didn't let up. Wherever a pattern of crime formed, he managed to track it to its source, leaving the police to play catch-up again. Embarrassingly, it was only after the fact that the police would discover their other lives. He, whoever "he" was, kept hunting down the scum that stalked New Zealand, the scum that hid behind innocent facades and put them in a long pine box. Some were saying that what he had done was not justice; others say that there should be more like him. She quietly agreed with the latter.

Megan finished her coffee, folded the paper neatly and then aligned it squarely with the edge of the bench. Her shift started in twenty minutes, so she grabbed her coat and headed for the door. Outside it was raining, again. Another typical winter's day in Auckland, New Zealand. Traffic was light for the early afternoon, which she thought was a blessing. Driving in city traffic was not her favourite past time.

She pulled into the station parking lot on Buscomb Avenue and locked her car as she got out. Megan walked in through the front doors and past the sullen receptionist towards the rear of the building. The vigilante's profile had been building for some time, but she had yet to come up with anything definitive to contribute and, thereby, giving the police a lead to follow. She pushed the door open to her office and was almost shoved in by Holmes, who had appeared behind her.

"You better have some news for me, Megan, and it better be good," he spat at her.

Megan walked behind the captain and closed the door. She proceeded to take her time removing her coat and scarf, taking care to hang them precisely on the coat rack in the corner of her office. She walked slowly towards and around the edge of her desk, completely ignoring Holmes. It wasn't until she was settled in her seat that she cast her eyes in his direction. She knew how to play his game and waited for him to go first.

"That's the seventh hit in as many months, and so far, you haven't given me shit to work with, Megan. What's the deal?"

Megan eyed Holmes, waiting for him to back down first before she answered.

"Well, Captain Holmes, first let's drop the talk of 'hits.' We only suspect a connection here—so far, the suspect has given me shit to work with. Evidence left at the scene is scarce"—she shot him a look—"especially after the number of people you throw at the crime scene have contaminated any that may have been left behind."

The captain clenched his jaw; he was not used to being talked back to, especially by a female colleague. Holmes dropped his gaze to the floor and smiled.

"Fair enough. How would you like to handle the next crime scene that involves this mongrel? Because you know there will be another." He stated this last part as if it were a foregone conclusion. Megan dropped her gaze to the desk and looked at a typewritten page in front of her.

"Cordon it off and let no one near it until I get there," she replied, knowing that it would get his back up. But that's what needed to happen. The captain looked at her hard.

"OK. Your call. Next time, you are the lead investigator. Don't screw this up, Megan, otherwise you will find yourself looking for another job." Megan held his gaze until he broke away and turned for the door. She knew Holmes was a good cop, but he didn't know shit about forensics. That was her field.

CHAPTER 5

I walked down Oriental Parade. A biting wind struck my face from the north, and my eyes began to water. The flight down had been bumpy, to say the least, and the landing had been rather exciting. I waited for twenty minutes for my contact to show, but he didn't. As I climbed into a cab, I received a call from him. Short and to the point as always, this is why I liked him. He told me he had an urgent job to take care of and would be home around midnight. I told him I would see him then.

As I approached the hotel, I slowed my pace and began looking for people sitting on park benches. If this guy was any good, he would see me coming—not that I was trying to hide myself. I was dressed conservatively. Jeans and a heavy jacket to combat the cold. It was dark and approaching eight, and I had just started rethinking my decision. In the end, I decided to go through with it. He may come in handy if I needed something.

I made my way down the street slowly, the ocean smashing against the rocks that formed the barrier along one side of the road. I saw the bench outside the hotel from a distance with nobody sitting on it. Disappointing.

Still, I would give the guy five minutes then walk away.

I stood with my nose into the wind and watched the lights flicker in the distance. The guy from the night before had entered my thoughts for some reason. Something he said before I pulled the trigger made me think. I quickly dismissed it; he got what he deserved.

I looked at my watch; he had another thirty seconds before I vanished into thin air. My eyes darted towards the park bench and saw someone sitting on it.

"Must be my guy," I mumbled. I walked towards the rocks on the edge of the road and looked out at the sea. He remained sitting there, no indication I'd been spotted. Slowly I made my way towards him; I wanted to come up from behind. No fancy strategy; it was just something I did out of habit. I walked towards him, keeping my eyes looking out over the harbour. It was a beautiful night, but cold as any other.

The guy leaned forward and looked up and down the street but couldn't see me; I was too far behind him. I made my way towards him slowly to check to see if he was carrying anything that could be used as a weapon. He wasn't.

"Rather trusting, aren't you?" I asked.

The guy turned around to face me. He was all of twenty something. As he stood up, I noticed he was not very tall either. I shoved my hands into the large pockets of my trench coat and wrapped my fingers around the roll of dollar coins. If it came to it, some passer-by was going to be able to have a free coffee in the morning. I kept my eyes on him as he moved slowly around the edge of the seat and stuck out his hand. I looked him up and down slowly then relaxed my grip on the roll.

"Dan," he said as a greeting when I shook his hand, not moving my eyes from his. There was hardness there, but also the enthusiasm of youth.

"You have five minutes."

Dan didn't waste his time. "Basically I'm a computer geek. I can get you access to damn near any electronic database you need," he stated. I looked hard at him and stayed quiet. I was not in the business of taking people on, didn't want a sidekick, but I could see a potential use.

"So what makes you think I can't?" I asked.

Dan thought about his answer. I could see it in his body language that he didn't want to insult me, which made him more genuine. What he came out with though made me think again. "I think I can do it faster."

He said it with confidence. His answer made the decision for me. "OK." I handed him a slip of paper with an address on it and a time. It was an abandoned warehouse in Hamilton. If he knew what he was doing, then he would be able to find me. I turned and walked back the way I came. My coat flapped in the breeze as the wind gusted past me. Without turning back, I said, "Don't be late."

Chapter 6

Maria Snijder sat on a bench in Jubilee Park. She was watching her two ten-year-old twin daughters as they ran across the soft grass. They were towing two kites they'd received as gifts. The wind was good for flying, and there were others in the distance too. She followed the kites as they soared high into the breeze and thought how much the three of them missed their dad, Kevin. Her husband had been killed one night as he drove home from work. A drunk driver had crossed the centre line and ploughed head-on into him. It killed him instantly, and had killed the heart of their family at the same time.

"Don't go too far!" she called out as the twins raced away under the winter sun. The girls ignored her and kept running as fast as their legs would allow.

It was one of the few days during the winter that broke the rain and allowed the sun to shine. Maria dropped her gaze to the ground beneath her feet and kicked her shoes off, then dug her toes into the soft grass. The sting of her husband's death had waned, but it was still there, bringing her down when she least expected it. All she wanted to remain were happy memories.

Her daughters, Donna and Kathy, were all that kept her sane. All that kept her wanting to wake up in the morning.

The twins ran towards a grove of trees near the northern end of the park. Their kites were soaring high in the sky. If Maria hadn't been watching the kites, she'd have seen them both suddenly stop, as if by some unheard comment between the two, and turn to watch their kites flutter in the breeze. They had run close to the grove, and the tumbling wind from the trees had caused their kites to dip and plummet towards the earth. They hit the ground one after the other. *Thud, thud.*

"Can I help you?" a voice asked from behind them.

The twins turned in unison to see a large man towering over them. He smiled cheerfully as though he did this every day, offering assistance to small children.

"No, our mum told us never to talk to strangers," Donna replied. She was only the eldest by ten minutes, but she still felt like the big sister.

The man towered over them, smiling politely. "Your mum is wise to teach you that. You never know who you might meet. My name is Jakob. What's yours?"

The twins remained silent and watched the man with careful eyes. After checking with her twin a moment, the eldest answered, "I'm Donna."

Kathy remained silent, watching the man in front of her. The man smiled and extended his hand to shake hers. Donna hesitated then placed her hand in the stranger's hand.

"DONNA, NO!" the scream came from behind. But by then it was too late.

Maria watched in horror as the tall man wrapped his fingers around her daughter's delicate hand in a vice like grip then picked her up in one easy motion. Maria was at least hundred feet from them as the horror scene unfolded before her. The man looked up suddenly and flashed her a grin that could only be described as sadistic. He tightened his grip and turned to run towards the grove of trees at the far end of the park.

Maria ran as fast as she could after the man but seemed to be losing ground with every step. Tears rolled down her cheeks. She screamed for him to stop, but the man kept running. Running hard.

It would be the last time she would see her daughter alive.

Chapter 7

Police surrounded the park and searched the cordoned area. Jubilee Park was a known hotspot for all sorts of criminal activity. Deals of all sorts could be struck in the relative privacy of the wood, but only a quick step to the main roads. What concerned the police about this brazen attack was that it had happened during daylight hours. Normally it was a ground for predators during the night and consequently was heavily patrolled, but not during the day.

Maria had given an accurate, but brief, description of the man she saw fleeing across the park with her daughter, but it also matched any one of a thousand people that could have been in the area at the time.

Megan arrived as dusk was approaching. This followed a mad dash down the highway, "but not too fast," she smiled to herself, after Captain Holmes had told her to get down to Hamilton. She was a leading forensic psychologist in the country, and her presence had been demanded. From the quick description of the crime, it sounded like another candidate for her favourite vigilante.

Megan stepped over the chain-link boundary fence to the park and walked slowly towards the roped-off area. She swept the scene, left to right, as she approached. Stopping a few yards short of the cordoned area, she took in her surroundings. A tall dark man with his hat pulled low over his eyes walked up to her.

"You can't be here, ma'am. Please get back to the boundary fence," the man stated this with the usual voice police used to convey authority. Megan ignored him and kept looking over his shoulder, and carefully around the area. Having had her first sweep, she started walking slowly towards the grove of trees, being careful to stay outside the cordon.

"Ma'am, I told you to get back. This is a crime scene, and we are—" "Contaminating it," Megan cut in. "What's your name, Officer?" "Loader," he replied.

Megan nodded, not really caring what the man's name was. That was the least of her worries. "OK, Officer Loader, I want you and your men out of there right now. Like you said, this is a crime scene, and forensics should be in there first to clear the scene. From what I can see, if there is any evidence to be gathered, it has most likely been destroyed by now." She looked towards the trees. The officer bunched his shoulders and was about to tell her in no uncertain terms that she had to be elsewhere, now.

"Constable, cool it. She has been sent here by the Serious Crime Unit," a voice yelled behind him. Loader clenched his jaw and stared at Megan. He turned and walked off. Another man in plain clothes walked up and greeted her.

"Megan, hello. Please forgive my overeager colleagues, they didn't know that you were requested to attend the crime scene. I'm Captain Waters." The man stuck his hand out.

Megan looked at him for a split second and shook his hand. It was a pleasantly firm handshake, and she returned in kind. Looking at the expanse of grass between the cones and the trees in the background, she asked, "What do we know about the man so far?"

Waters turned and looked in the same direction.

"A male, about six feet tall. Blond hair and of solid build. He was wearing a red sports jacket and blue denim jeans. That was the description we managed to get from the mother. She had a good look, poor woman, so there's no immediate reason to doubt her accuracy." Megan looked back at Captain Waters.

"I take it Holmes has told you that I need full cooperation from you and your attending officers?" she asked. Waters nodded and lifted the cordon tape so Megan could slip underneath.

"Where was the mother sitting when the abduction happened?" she asked. Waters turned and pointed at a park bench in the distance.

"There, she was watching her daughters fly kites. She remembers watching the kites fall to the ground, then looking back up and seeing a man dressed in a red jacket talking to them. That was when she stood and ran for them. The perp allegedly shook the hand of one of the girls and picked her up then ran for the trees at the end of the park. Maria gave chase but couldn't catch him. . She lost him in the trees." Megan focused on the trees from where she was standing.

"Is this exactly where the incident took place?" she asked. Waters nodded and looked away.

"The guy must have been fit to run that distance at a full sprint carrying an extra seventy or eighty pounds," Megan said.

Jakob Richardson was walking with an air of superiority down the foot path of the road which ran alongside Jubilee Park. He was taking a huge risk in doing so, but he knew that no one had seen him. Even so, he had disguised his appearance by changing his hair colour. An obvious trick, but it was surprising how often it worked. He also wore sunglasses, had a hat pulled low over his eyes, and a scarf wrapped around his neck.

He hunched his shoulders into the thick winter coat as he cast his eyes left; surveying the scene he had been a part of the day before. He knew the police would never catch him. He was too good. Always one step ahead of the game. That's what he kept telling himself as he glanced at the swarm of uniforms covering every inch of ground between the park bench and the grove of trees. He stopped and surveyed the scene. Looking at his watch, he remembered the rush he had felt as he ran for the trees carrying the girl. A sick smile spread over his face.

"Excuse me, sir?"

He shook his head with a start and spun around to see a woman walking towards him. Instantly he was captivated by her beauty. Adrenaline flooded into his veins as the rush he had already been feeling surged tenfold. Jakob turned around to face her. "Yes?" he answered.

"We are conducting an investigation here. Would you mind if I asked you a couple of questions?" The woman was watching him closely. Jakob wouldn't have noticed at that point. He nodded, his eyes taking in her tall and slender appearance.

"Are you from around here?" the woman asked. Jakob nodded again. "Yes, I live just down the street," he lied. He followed the woman's hand as she reached inside her jacket and removed a small ring-bound pad and a pen. He was watching close enough to notice she carried a badge and a gun. But that wasn't what caught his breath. The plump swell of her breast made him choose her. He couldn't believe his luck! Couldn't believe he had found someone so quickly. He was becoming bored with the other two and needed some new blood.

"Do you walk this way often?" she asked again.

"Most days," he replied. "I usually come this way when I need to go to town for whatever reason." His head suddenly cleared, and he flashed his best prize-winning smile.

The woman made a note in her book then looked him straight in the eye. Her inquisitive gaze made him feel rather uncomfortable.

"What time did you happen to walk past here yesterday?" she asked suddenly and casually, looking down at her pad again. Jakob almost fell for it, almost got caught in her well-laid trap. If he hadn't been ready for it, he surely would have turned a corner that he did not want to go down.

"I never said I walked down here yesterday," he countered with a sly smirk.

The woman looked up slowly then back down at her book. He wanted her to ask him if he had walked past yesterday. But the woman just nodded and put the pad back in the hidden pocket of her jacket. Jakob managed to catch another glimpse of her clothed body. He flushed.

"One more question, sir. I need some contact details if anything else comes up."

The question caught Jakob off guard.

"Norman Octavia. Fifty Tramway Road." He repeated it back again to make sure she got it right. The cop nodded then slowly turned away. He noticed she didn't bother writing it down. Jakob stood for a second longer then walked hastily up the road towards the town centre.

Megan walked back towards the cordon after having questioned the man who said his name was Norman. She had her doubts about what he'd said though. Megan had the feeling she had just been lied to but couldn't figure out why as she approached Captain Waters.

"Can you send me a copy of all the evidence that has been found here?" she asked.

"Certainly can. Anything to help get that little girl back," he said. He knew that the first twenty-four hours were the most critical. Any and all information sharing at this time was a good thing. She removed the small pad from her jacket and scribbled down a name and address.

Megan handed him a slip of paper with the man's details on it. "Could you possibly run this through the system as well?" Waters took the slip of paper and turned it over to look at it.

"Norman Octavia. I'll check it out and get back to you with the list of evidence so far. As yet unverified evidence, you understand."

Megan nodded then turned and walked off towards the boundary fence. She stepped over the chain and turned to look back at the crime scene. She had a feeling things were about to get a lot worse. This crime was bad enough to attract attention, both of the good and the not-so-good variety.

Chapter 8

"Shut the hell up!" Jakob screamed, but the noise only served to make the girl cry harder. He was beginning to regret bringing her here, stealing her from her safe life. The constant whining was becoming unbearable. Jakob flicked the lights off, and the cries intensified again. He flicked them back on and focused on Donna with a hard stare. She was curled up in a tight ball and jammed into the corner of the closest steel cage. Melanie stood behind her, eyeing Jakob.

"Leave her alone," she pleaded. "She's only ten for god's sake." Jakob flicked his gaze to Melanie then back to Donna.

"When I come back tomorrow, the crying had better have stopped," he said eventually. No softness in this voice. He flicked the light off and walked for the door in the dark. As he cracked it open, he stopped in the dull sliver of light that shone through.

"Because if it hasn't—if you don't stop screaming—you will never see your mother and sister again."

The door slammed shut, and the three captives were plunged into darkness. Melanie opened her eyes wide but could not see a thing. She couldn't remember the last time she had seen sunlight. If she had to guess, she thought it had been about a week that she had been captive. The girl had only been here one night, and it had been a sleepless night for all of them. Melanie had tried to talk to Donna, but she kept crying. Finally she fell asleep, and the silence became audible. Melanie turned to Anna.

"Are you OK?" Melanie asked.

Anna nodded in the darkness but didn't answer. She couldn't. Jakob had almost strangled the life from her in a fit of rage resulting from some perceived slight. It had only been Melanie's pleading with him that had saved her life. Anna had begun to see stars before he had released her. His crushing grip had caused her to lose her voice. Five purple marks had made themselves apparent the next day. It had been three days since, and her voice still only came out as a hoarse croak. Anna hadn't eaten anything since that day, swallowing was still too painful, and she was beginning to feel weak because of it.

"Just get some sleep. He'll be back soon, and we need to keep her quiet." She nodded towards Donna, who had finally settled to a quiet whimper. She lay down on the cold, damp floor.

Her dreams made her restless, short as they were. She could see herself standing in a field of daisies with the sun shining down on her bare shoulders. She turned a full circle; the field seemed to run on forever in every direction. The air was fresh, she was free and alive.

Then she panicked. Everything looked the same. She had the feeling of being trapped even though she was not caged. The field closed in on her, and she awoke with a scream trembling on the edge of her lips.

When she opened her eyes, the lights were on, and Jakob stood at the door to her cage. He was staring at her with the same sort of look he might use on a misbehaving pup. Melanie sat up abruptly, her mouth dropped open.

"I told you that if she was making any noise when I returned then she would not see her mother and sister alive again." Jakob turned to look at the young girl who was standing in the centre of the room, wide-eyed, a cloth gag tied tightly in her mouth. Her hands were bound at her back.

"You could have saved her, Melanie. You should have saved her!" he was screaming. He jabbed a finger at her. "Now it is your fault that she has to die."

Jakob stood stone-still in the middle of the cave, staring intensely at her. Melanie quickly climbed to her feet and rushed to the edge of the cage. Her hand shot out past Jakob towards the young girl perched precariously on a rickety old stool.

"No, Jakob, please, you can't do this. She doesn't deserve to die," Melanie pleaded, but knowing that it was hopeless. This guy had already done enough to prove how serious he was. Jakob only grinned and shook his head.

"Not this time, you slut! Not this time!" he yelled. Jakob turned and walked swiftly towards the chair. As he reached the young girl, he casually stuck his hand out, clipping her shoulder and pushing her off balance. A muffled squeal escaped her throat as the chair tipped over, sending her tumbling.

Horror flooded through Melanie as the thick rope snapped tight around the little girl's throat, stopping her toes inches from the floor.

Chapter 9

After a night filled with dreams, Jakob pulled the steel door open to the dungeon buried beneath the surface of the earth after he had descended two flights of stairs to reach it. The hinges whined in protest as he struggled to make a gap large enough for him to fit through.

He stepped into the chamber and pushed the door close behind him. He could hear the sound of heavy scared breathing in the darkness. The air was rank with dirt and waste, but the fear seemed to overwhelm both. He reached into his pocket and pulled out a shiny but worn silver Zippo lighter. He struck the flint, and a small but strong flame danced off the wick. This lit up the immediate area in a pale yellow colour. It could penetrate no further than ten feet in front of Jakob. But he knew where he was going.

"Good evening, ladies," he said to the darkness in a childish tone. Anna began whimpering in the darkness towards the far end of the chamber.

"No, that's no way to greet your host." The whimpering died, and silence took over. Slowly, one of the girls stood and looked as far as she could towards the light at the end of the chamber.

"Hello, Master," she said, hoping the other would follow suit. They had seen what would happen if they did not obey him. The ten-year-old girl had been a testimony to his disgusting behaviour. The chamber remained silent. Jakob had three cages bolted to the wall and locked them with brand new combination locks. The two girls he had locked away in them would be secure. He walked towards a string that was hanging from the ceiling. From the flame of the lighter, it was seemingly hanging in mid-air. He reached up and grasped the plastic end and pulled it. Harsh light radiated from fittings high in the natural roof of the cavern.

"OK. We have lots to prepare for. A new arrival will be joining us soon. We need to tidy this filthy mess up before her . . . " He trailed off and found himself looking at the door embedded in rock at the far end of the room. He knew what was behind that door. She was behind it. That stupid, stupid little girl, he never should have taken her. Jakob turned away in disgust. It ate at him. All the others had been obedient; all the others had done as he had told them. Everyone but her.

She had done nothing but cry all the time she was here. He was a tolerant person, but he couldn't take it couldn't take the constant whining. Even the others had told her to shut up, but she kept wailing. Eventually he had snapped and dragged her out of the cage by her hair kicking and screaming. He had held her up in front of the other two girls and told them this is what would happen if they decided to torment him. Jakob had lifted Donna up until the tips of her toes were scraping the dirt floor.

Now he looked in the direction of the door and remembered what she had been like. What she had tasted like. He likened it to strawberries and ice cream. His favourite dish when he was her age.

"Yes, we need to arrange this to her liking," he stated for the benefit of the remaining two girls. Jakob walked up to the first cage and gently grabbed the lock. He looked at the girl huddling at the back of the cage. Her arms and face were covered in dried blood. Dirty blue and black bruises peppered her skin and disappeared under her ragged clothes. Jakob looked at her, menace in his face.

"Now, Melanie, are we going to have any problems again, or are you going to behave yourself and do as I say?"

Melanie locked a fierce gaze at him and nodded. She had lost track of how long she had been down there, in hell. But she knew, one way or another, she would get out or die trying.

"I'll behave," she said quietly.

"Good. I want you to start by cleaning out the end cell. Then you can pick up any rubbish that may be lying around." His voice was casual, but certainly not to be taken lightly. He dialled the numbers into the lock, then pulled the lock from the metal loops and slammed the door back. She was expecting the noise, but she still found herself jumping at the sound. As he stepped forward, filling the doorway, he drew a pistol and levelled it at her chest, a breath caught in her throat.

"Up." He motioned with the pistol. "And don't get any stupid ideas."

He directed Melanie to the rear cage, then sat on an oil drum and watched her carefully, evaluating.

The other girl was sprawled on the floor, her filthy legs twisted at a sharp angle. Jakob was certain she was dead, but he couldn't be bothered finding out for sure. She was no longer useful to him. Not able to do as she was told. He thought when the smell became too much, he would have lovely little Melanie do something about it.

Chapter 10

Megan walked into the tall, thick brush of the wetlands of the Hauraki Plains with a digital camera slung around her neck. The wetlands stretched for miles. They were huge flood plains, almost always covered in water during the winter. It was only a local hunter that had chanced upon the body that had alerted the authorities; otherwise, it would have remained undiscovered, probably until the summer month's maybe never to be discovered.

They had barely started the investigation into Donna's abduction when her body was found. They had only just begun to look towards a ransom demand. Megan followed the new muddy track, which had been beaten down by numerous people walking to and from the body. As per her orders, a proper cordon had been set up around the area, and no one had been allowed near it until she arrived. What they had found repulsed even her.

"Jesus Christ," she muttered to herself. Even from a distance, she could see that this had been staged for someone's benefit. The body was wrapped in a plastic sheet and tied up with thick cord. The killer had buried her half in and half out of the dirt. Blood smeared the inside of the plastic sheet, making identification difficult from a distance.

Megan turned and looked at Captain Waters, her face almost cracking with the various emotions a crime like this managed to stir in everyone. Sorrow, disgust, hate—they all had a place. Waters looked at her, then back to the girl buried in the dirt. Lifting the tape, Megan stepped underneath and followed the path. She stopped a few feet short of the body.

Reluctantly, she lifted the camera and took the first of a multitude of shots. As she did this, she made extensive notes. A trained observer, she took in the disturbed grass and mud, taking into account all imprints and any evidence of movement or action she could see. As she slowly circled around the body sticking out of the mud for the last time, she signalled to Captain Waters that he could send in a team to extract her from her grave.

She stepped back and watched as they dug the mud from around her waist and down around her legs. The body fell forward and splashed into the muddy water. Carefully, as if the young girl were still alive, some officers lifted the small body from her watery grave and carried her to a waiting ambulance. In a few hours she'd pay a visit to the ME. Megan didn't think there'd be any problems determining the cause of death.

"I hope you find something we can use, Detective," Waters said as she walked past.

She was following the ambulance crew as they readied themselves for the trip back to town. Megan stopped and turned to face him. "If he's left something, I'll find it." He watched her go, and then followed her to the roadside.

The ride back to Auckland was slow and painful. The wet countryside rolled by as the rain beat down on the windscreen, the wipers fighting a losing battle to keep it clear. She didn't hear the thump of the wipers or the relentless noise of the rain; her mind was somewhere else.

A place where the sun was shining and the warmth kept the killer at bay.

Who was he? She imagined the man standing before her. Forcing him on his knees, his head bowed towards the ground. She wanted to hurt him, to kill him. Make him feel what this beautiful young girl had gone through. The rage that built so easily in crimes like these flooded her for a second. In her mind, she grabbed him by his hair and wrenched his head back at an almost unnatural angle. What looked back at her was nothing, his face bare.

She was chasing a ghost.

Megan pushed through the stainless steel doors that lead to the morgue. It was late, and she could feel her eyelids beginning to droop dangerously. After being shown to where the small body lay, she peeled back the white sheet then gazed down at the small girl. Even in death, her face was twisted and contorted in pain. A thick mark ran around the circumference of her neck, the strands of the rope clearly visible in the skin. Megan shifted her hand to her mouth and stifled a yawn. She knew she had to stay focused for the exam, but her mind screamed silently for sleep.

Nothing unusual, apart from her actual death, was found with the girl. She was perfectly normal and healthy. The time of death had been about forty eight hours ago at the rate rigor mortis had set in. Overnight temperatures would be sourced later to make a more accurate judgement. Thin cut marks consistent with small synthetic rope ran around the tops of her wrists, the burns indicating she had struggled before she fell.

Megan wrote her own notes and logged everything on a small laptop. She was building a comprehensive package to give to Captains Holmes and Waters, but so far, nothing obvious had been found on the girl indicating a link to the killer. She hadn't been raped. As far as she could tell, he had hardly touched her. There was some light bruising on her upper arms, but other than that, nothing.

Megan sighed and draped the white sheet back over the body. They had found virtually nothing. Megan thought either this guy was very careful, or he just liked to watch his captives squirm. She shut her laptop down and stuffed it into her bag, followed by her hardcopy notes. Flicking the lights off as she left, Megan made her way to the car park.

Weariness was beginning to take a serious hold of her, and she needed to get home. Knowing she probably shouldn't be driving; she wound the windows down and turned some god-awful radio station up loud to help keep her awake. The short drive to Rosebank was faster than usual; at two o'clock in the morning, traffic was light. Megan pulled her car off the road and into the driveway. Locking up behind her, she turned and staggered bleary-eyed towards her front door. She slipped the key into the lock and pushed the door open. She pulled her badge and gun out, and then laid them carefully on the table next to the kitchen. Megan looked at the stove then the fridge and made her mind up to go to bed hungry. Tomorrow was only four hours away. She switched the lights off and crawled into bed.

Jakob sat in the shadows on the opposite side of the street, about a hundred metres from her driveway. He watched the lights go out as he played with a lock of the young girl's hair. He lifted it to his face and breathed in the scent.

Young and fresh.

In total he had seven locks of hair. He began to wonder what the detective's hair would smell like. What her skin would smell like. Wondered what she looked like naked and screaming in pain.

Chapter 11

Melanie hung from her wrists. The chains were biting into her skin, allowing blood to trickle down her forearms. Her fingers had started to go numb under the tension, only the balls of her feet supported her weight. Jakob had left her like that while he went out. He didn't trust her. Her shoulders screamed in agony as sweat dripped from her forehead. She had never felt pain like it before.

The door cracked open and squealed as Jakob pushed it wide. He stepped into the room and closed it, plunging the room into darkness once again. "Well done, six hours, I'm impressed."

He walked twelve paces to the middle of the cavern and pulled the string. The room flashed into light, the sudden brightness almost blinding Melanie. She had been hanging in the darkness for what seemed like eternity. Her tired eyes found Jakob as he walked towards her; she wouldn't look at him directly in the eyes. His face was expressionless, like a stone mask. She tried to remain still and calm, not wanting to provoke him, but the pain began to overtake her again.

"Let me go!" she screamed.

Jakob looked at her, and then slowly shook his head. "You know I can't do that." He grinned at her.

Jakob turned away and quickly disappeared into the darkness. He returned a minute later with a large kitchen knife. It looked like the one her granddad used to carve the ham at Christmas. He held it up for her to see, and it glinted in the dull light from the single bulb. He walked up to her and ran it slowly down the side of her face. She twitched under the cold steel, and the blade left a shallow cut in the soft flesh of her cheek. She screwed her eyes shut and turned her head away. Jakob stepped back. The evil grin spread back across his lips.

"Don't worry, you aren't going to die tonight," he said as he walked around behind her. Leaping forward, he grabbed a handful of hair and wrenched her head back so she was looking up at her swollen purple wrists. He lifted the blade up and brought it slowly across the soft skin of her throat.

"But don't worry, when it is your time to go, you won't feel a thing."

Melanie could feel his hot acrid breath on her neck, and she tried to turn away but couldn't. The knife disappeared, and Jakob let her hair go. She waited for him to do something. As the seconds of silence grew, an increasing panic flooded through her. She couldn't hear or see him. Melanie tried to turn around but could only see darkness.

Then the cackle echoed out of the darkness. The same cackle she had heard before.

It happened so fast she didn't have time to scream. The knife sliced her clothing away, falling at her feet by an unseen hand. There was a shuffle behind her, and she felt his hot breath on her neck again.

This time she knew what was going to happen.

Chapter 12

I stood in the shadows watching Megan go into her house. The lights flicked on and off as she moved through it towards what I guessed was her bedroom. She had been turning up at the murder scenes of people of ill repute like a shadow, and I was beginning to wonder why she was doing it. Was she assigned to tracking me? Or was it coincidence?

I knew that everywhere I had been, I hadn't left any clues, but then again, I got the feeling she wasn't looking too hard either. This made me interested. A fellow soul? A cop? I stood in the shadows debating with myself, wondering what was going to happen next. I looked up at the cloudless sky then back at her house. The lights had gone out, and darkness had settled in.

It was then, in the quiet, I could feel something out of place. It wasn't anything obvious, but something began to gnaw at me. I couldn't put my finger on it. I looked up and down the street then returned to the house.

I had been watching her movements for what seemed like an eternity, but was probably closer to weeks, and began to wonder if she could be useful. It needled me all the way back home. Something wasn't right, but it still eluded me. Eventually I gave up on chasing a shadow and lifted the screen on my laptop. I logged on to see if there was anything useful being pushed around the Internet.

I had waited twenty minutes before someone decided to talk to me. It slowly dawned on me that it was some kid playing around on Mum and Dad's computer, not realising who he was talking to. I told him to find someone else, blocked him, and kept waiting.

I was about to flag it when a question popped up. I had all my tracks covered, but the question made me stop. It wasn't your usual introductory line.

Are you still there? It asked. I looked at it and formulated my answer before I typed it. I hadn't talked to anyone in the chat room, and the kid had logged off and disappeared.

I'm still here, I wrote.

Good. Just wanted to make sure.

I looked at the message and didn't recognise the user name. *Who the fuck are you?* I mumbled to myself as I waited for a response. I grabbed a pen and a notepad then wrote down the user name: JR44.

I've been tracking your progress Spangle 36. I know you are not a female with a large chest sitting at your computer looking for companionship. I believe I have seen your work Spangle 36, I know what you do. It doesn't take a genius to see through you.

I read the message again. It didn't take a genius to figure out that not everyone on the net was telling the truth either although he was also right about having seen my work. A lot of people had seen my work. It was all over the television and through the newspapers. I decided to play ignorant about the situation.

I honestly have no idea what you are talking about, I replied, knowing that it was complete bullshit. It didn't take long for the reply to come through, and as I expected, he saw straight through it.

You really should stop lying Spangle 36. It will get you nowhere. Did you like the piece I put on exhibition?

I read the message again and decided to drop the act.

I can't say that I have seen any of your handiwork; I typed and then hit Enter. The sentence appeared on the screen in front of me and then the cursor indicated that JR44 was typing a response.

That's a shame. I've done, some people would say, some really arty stuff. Maybe you should look it up, or maybe you have already heard of some of it.

No I don't think I have. Your kind tends not to last too long, I replied, and as I had hoped, he took the bait.

HAHA. I take it that we don't last too long because you are here to stop us. Good luck Spangle 36, keep dreaming, the message flashed up. But it also indicated he was writing again. I sat back and waited for the sicko to send his next message.

Surely you must have seen my artwork; I call it Winter's Bloom.? It stated more than asked. I had, and the police report had made my stomach turn. The sick fuck had hung her. Hung a ten-year-old girl. Her name was Donna Snijder. I clenched my fist as I thought about what hell she must have gone through. My blood began to simmer.

I decided to kill the connection, not wanting to get into a heated argument with this sick fuck over the net. Sitting in my seat for a few minutes, I started to stew over the conversation that had just taken place. It took willpower not to let myself get worked up—it was never a good idea for me to get carried away. I stood up abruptly, grabbed my coat, and headed for the door.

Chapter 13

J akob sat in an Internet café on Queen Street, down near the waterfront. It was a great view from the window, and he didn't look out of place among the other die-hard WOW geeks sitting in front of their computers.

He had taken a huge risk taunting Emery and knew that it could quite easily turn around and bite him big time if he wasn't cautious. Spontaneity and improvisation at this stage of the game was risky. Jakob deleted the browser history and any tracking cookies that had popped up.

He had been watching the guy one newspaper had labelled as "vigilante" for months. Never any evidence, it was only recently a local reporter's well- trained nose had hinted at the possible connections. Jakob knew one day their paths would probably cross. The type of people being found meant that his current habits put him in a group titled "High Risk." In his mind, it was capitalised just that way. *High Risk*. But Jakob was smart. If he could control the situation, it would all pan out on his terms.

His mind returning back to the basement, he remembered he had left Melanie alone tonight, locked in her cage. She was growing thinner by the day. He supposed he should bring her some food, but he reminded himself that she had to earn it first. Task then reward. That's how it worked. Unless he decided elsewise. Food was a luxury that he would give her if *he* desired. Jakob had set Melanie a task. Not a particularly difficult one by his standards, but one he was sure that she would not be able to complete. Or more to the point, would not want to complete. He had spelt out to her the consequence of not doing as she was told, but secretly he hoped that she wouldn't go through with it. He wanted to see her suffer a little. Just a little. Hold control of her pain, increase it slowly, and then release her from that pain just as she is about to give up. That emotional control was addictive and overrode any compassion he may have once had.

Jakob walked out of the café and turned his collar up against the biting southerly that had sprung up. He stepped onto the footpath and began walking towards the city centre. He felt an electric mixture of fear, power, and lust that had him jumpy. He felt like finding someone to spend the night with. Get it out of his system; let him focus on the work in progress. As he walked, head down, he began to think about the cop from Hamilton. He had found out everything he could about her. Her age, where she was from, and, more importantly, where she lived. He had already been to her house once. He remembered walking through the section. He thought it was a mess, but then again, not everyone was as tidy and under control as he was.

A hand reached out of his peripheral vision and stopped him from hitting a person walking in the opposite direction. Jakob looked up, startled, and locked eyes with the man standing in front of him. Tall and very well-dressed, an arrogant flare erupted in his eyes. He had a coat slung oh-so-casually over his shoulder. The man stood his ground and waited expectantly for Jakob to move out of his way. Jakob quickly looked at the ground and moved to the right.

"Sorry," he mumbled as he walked past, and continued to head down the street. The man didn't acknowledge the mumbled apology, although Jakob didn't stick around to hear if he had. He kept walking towards the waterfront and didn't look back. He turned the corner at the end of the street, to more people out socialising and shopping down towards the viaduct. He suddenly stopped and clenched his fists, angry with himself. He'd been bested. He'd just conceded to a man on the street, some random piece of trash that he knew, quite rightly was clearly above.

"How fucking dare he." A couple stared cautiously at him as they strode past, heading in the opposite direction. Jakob shot them a filthy sneer, but the couple didn't look away. He ignored them and began to move down the footpath, his movements stiff with a building anger. He was thinking how much he would like to sneak up behind the man on the street and ram a knife through the back of his neck. The thought went a long way to easing the suffering his ego was feeling, but as far as he was concerned, not far enough.

He had unfinished business with society, and unfinished business with people who had torn him down. He'd been stripped of dignity, publicly humiliated. Made him the butt of their jokes and used him as a scapegoat. And he'd let them. And the girls were worse. He hated girls; they always made him feel devalued made him feel like a lesser human being.

He stopped and scoffed at himself. What was he thinking; they made him feel like something they'd scrape off their diamond-encrusted high heels. Jakob could feel the familiar cloud beginning to settle around him. He took comfort in the fact that he was stronger than they were. And that was something he needed to show them, even if it meant hurting them.

Reason said that it was the only way to make them understand, to train them, to make them see. They were nothing compared to him, to what he had become. He was the master of his world, and if he so desired, he was the master of their world too. He knew he couldn't be stopped.

CHAPTER 14

Melanie sat in the corner of her cage sobbing uncontrollably, the door wide open. She hadn't moved since Jakob had left the underground prison. He had told her, before he left, that he wanted the cave spotless by the time he returned. Three buckets of water stood in the far end of the cavern, next to a mop. On the bench beside it lay various tools. Ones Jakob had become proficient in using to terrify her.

The palms of her hands covered her face, but still she chanced a peek at the grisly site of Anna's body in the cage next to her. Tiny fragments of flesh lay splattered on the dirt floor, and pooled blood had crept under the lower wire strands of Melanie's cage. The images she had witnessed and the screams she'd heard assaulted her like horrible nightmares every time she closed her eyes, whether it was night time or not.

He had starved Anna until she was too weak to fight back. She could barely raise a hand to defend herself. This had made her easier to handle while he took to her body with a skill saw. He had completely torn her to pieces. Melanie hadn't stopped screaming, even after he had left. But before he had, Jakob had told her explicitly to have the mess cleaned up before he got back.

Her head remained in her hands. She had no idea how long he had been gone or how long she had been like that. All she could see in the darkness was the little girl swinging at the end of a rope and Anna struggling as Jakob cut her legs off. Her mind relentlessly churned through these images in a sickeningly detailed way, and her thoughts regularly returned to thinking about what he may do to her.

And when at last she removed her hands and opened her eyes, the images turned into reality.

Chapter 15

J erry drove the Envirowaste truck slowly down the narrow alleyway of a side street. It was one of his inner-city stops during his weekly rounds. He didn't like driving down here; he had to fold the wing mirrors in to avoid ripping them off as he gently pushed the truck down towards the bin at the end. Why they couldn't find a more convenient place to locate the bin, he would never know. But here he was, Tuesday morning, negotiating the narrow alleyway to get to the bin. He looked left then right and swung out across the street to line up on the entrance. He paused to lean across to swing the mirrors in, made sure again that he was dead in the centre, and moved in to the alleyway.

Rubbish lay scattered around the edges of the buildings, blown there by strong winds. Jerry wound down his window, and a blast of cold air hit him. It had the smell of decaying rubbish intermixed with the stale warm smell of air-conditioning exhaust. He slowed as he neared the bin then braked, stopping six feet short of it.

"Damn it," he muttered. In front of the large bin, lying on its side was a shopping trolley. Jerry had asked them repeatedly to keep the bin clear of any and all obstacles, and repeatedly they had ignored his requests. Even a thinly veiled threat by his manager to the lessees of the bin had fallen on deaf ears.

Jerry pushed his door open, and it slammed against the brick wall, adding another dent to its already scarred complexion. He squeezed through the tiny gap and landed heavily on the concrete surface. Wind tore at his back as he moved past the truck towards the front. Jerry grabbed the trolley's handle in his leather-gloved hand and lifted it back onto its wheels. It wasn't until it was right side up that he noticed a deep red, almost black, coating on most of the stainless steel wirework of the basket. He inspected it more closely, squinting as he leaned in towards it.

It was then he realised that he was looking at blood. Jerry recoiled away, slipped backwards on the slick concrete surface and sent the trolley crashing into the dumpster. The trolley hit the side of the bin with a thud; the sound told Jerry instantly that it was full. He scrambled to his feet and warily moved towards the bin. Stopping midway with his hand outstretched, Jerry pulled it back telling himself to stop. He didn't need to know what was in there. He didn't need this crap. He turned to walk away, but he had to know, had to find out what was in there. Carefully he lifted the green lid then quickly slammed it shut. His eyes jammed shut, and he bent over in two, vomiting on the concrete.

Megan walked towards the cordon tape. A truck blocked her view of the waste bin at the end of the tiny alleyway. Police milled around the scene but stayed away from the roped-off area. They had been told, in no uncertain terms, by Captain Holmes to stay out of it until she had arrived. Megan slipped under the tape and walked slowly down the gentle gradient towards the rear of the truck. It was quiet, only the noise of the nearby motorway could be heard. She looked down either side of the truck and slipped down the narrow gap without touching anything.

Megan reached the front and could instantly smell something rotten. The truck being such a tight fit had all but stopped the wind from getting to the waste bin and dispersing the smell. Consequently the stench hit her like a sledgehammer. She recoiled and placed her hand over her mouth.

"Oh god," she choked out. Megan stepped closer to the bin and slowly lifted the lid. The bloated body parts lay on the top of a pile of garbage. Rotting food added to the vile stench that drifted from the bin. Megan pushed the lid fully back and looked carefully around the scene.

The victim was female, that much she could tell. As for the cause of death, she had no idea, but she was sure a guess of massive blood loss wouldn't be far wrong. The victim's legs lay next to the torso, twisted together in a knot. The body had been mutilated; a large number of deep jagged cuts could be seen running from her neck right down to her pelvis. The nature of the wounds indicated to her that she was dealing with someone who had issues with women. She turned away from the bin and looked at the front of the truck. Megan knew of this kind of person all too well.

"What did you find, Detective?" Captain Holmes asked as Megan returned to the top of the alleyway. She looked down at the smooth surface of the street then back at Holmes.

"I think it's the work of the same guy that killed the girl we found in the swamp."

Holmes eyed her. "What makes you say that?"

She hadn't told anyone about her past, but she knew a serial killer when she saw one. Megan hesitated before answering. "I've seen this kind of behaviour before." She didn't want to give away any more.

Holmes let out a small snort, but remained silent while he stared at her. "Sir, what would you like us to do?" another officer asked. Holmes turned to face him, turning his back to Megan.

"Get that truck out of there and extract the body to the morgue. Bag everything else." He then turned and faced her again. "I'm assuming, of course, that it's all right with you? If we go in there and do our job?" His voice dripping sarcasm. Rather than answer, Megan turned away and walked across the street.

Jakob watched the show from the fifth-floor window of an apartment building. He knew what was in that bin. He knew the instant the truck turned down the alleyway that it would be found. He knew the instant it was found that the police would be called and Megan would turn up.

He had watched her intently until she disappeared behind the truck, returning five minutes later. Her shoulders were slumped, and her body language said everything he needed to hear. She had disappeared from his view, but he could still feel her. She was there, out of sight, but still he watched.

Jakob grew bored as an hour passed. He had been in the room since first light, knowing he wouldn't be disturbed. It was a new apartment block being built and was only partially finished. Stretching, and in need of stimulation, Jakob stood up and turned for the door. As he walked down the uncarpeted hallway, he thought about Anna. She hadn't been particularly pretty, rather ordinary in fact. What he did like about her was that she was so submissive. He had completely owned her. He even told her when she could die, and she had gone without saying a word.

Until the blade of the saw touched her skin.

A cheerful grin spread over his face as he thought about the look of horror in her eyes. He savoured that feeling. Loved it. And it made him hard just thinking about what he was going to do to go further, past it. But for now he was satisfied. For now he could wait until the time was right for him and Megan to meet.

Chapter 16

Dan drove to the address written on the piece of paper that Emery had given him. It was in an industrial area of Hamilton. He read the warning sign hanging on the fence as he pulled up next to it. It stated the building was about to be demolished and entry was only under permission of the city council. Dan looked past the sign at the building itself. It was old and showed advanced signs of decay. It was basically only the brick-and-mortar structure that had been left; everything else had been stripped out.

Dan stepped out of the car, into the puddle of light from a street lamp, and looked up and down the wire fence. There was some light from the moon, so the street lamp didn't offer much more in the way of visibility. He couldn't see an obvious entry point anywhere, so he checked again that no one was watching, to scale the fence as quickly as he could. He landed on the other side and ran for the building. The night was cold and damp, and the long weeds between the cracked asphalt soaked his cuffs. He began to wonder if Emery was playing him for an idiot. Quickly, he walked into the front entrance. Rubbish lay scattered everywhere the remains of the old and dying being removed to make way for the new.

Dan walked a dozen steps into the darkness and spun around. A chilly wind blew through the building, swirling damp dust and paper with it. He pulled a small but powerful flashlight from his pocket and flicked it on and instantly picked up a table in the middle of the large area of what he assumed was a warehouse of some sort. Even Dan, more used to simulated role play than real-life adventure, could see that this had been deliberately arranged so that it wouldn't be missed. Slowly he walked towards it, sweeping the light from left to right as he went looking for anything else out of the ordinary.

He reached the table and found a brand-new laptop sitting on it. Dan sat at the chair and carefully lifted the screen. Like a blue eye in the gloom, it blinked, blinked again, and greeted him. The screen was unembellished with only three icons on it, a My Computer, a Documents folder, and an Internet browser icon. Instinctively, Dan clicked on the documents folder to see if there was anything that could be useful. It was empty.

"Not surprising" he thought.

He clicked the explorer icon, and the screen brought up an Internet search engine. He typed in something random to see if the link had been established. It came back with six million hits in under half a second.

"OK . . . so this isn't a set up," he mumbled. Dan looked around the dark cavern of the warehouse. He could hear nothing but the sounds of a restless city in the background.

"Let's see where I can find you."

A small surge of adrenaline touched his blood. This whole setup felt dangerous, something out of one of those gangster movies where the computer guy always gets taken out. Not knowing where else to start, he entered keywords for local and national crime reports. The screen showed him fifty thousand hits in under 0.3 of a second. Dan clicked on the first item of the list. It was an article about a gang-related offence that saw two patched members of a local motorcycle gang murdered in broad daylight in a turf war with a rival gang. It happened in the middle of a small town known for violence and disruption by the local gangs. The mayor was quoted as saying that he and the police force were committed to removing the problems that had forced residents of the small town to leave.

Dan read the article but could see nothing that could possibly be related to who he was looking for. He opened the next article; it was about a homicide that had happened recently. A little girl had been found half buried in the Hauraki flood plains. Her cause of death had been suppressed, believed to be due to the violent nature of the crime.

Dan read a quote from the captain in charge. "We are doing everything within our power to locate the perpetrator and bring him to justice."

"Yeah, that sounds like a typical line they use for the media. They don't know much," he mumbled to himself as he kept reading. He closed the article and opened the third. It was written by a reporter he knew of—he was good, but tended to dramatize stories to boost his ratings. Dan read the headline aloud.

"Reformed child molester murdered." He looked around the empty warehouse again then continued reading the article. He got to the paragraph where it stated that the man had died from a gunshot wound to the forehead. A second shot was fired from point-blank range into the man's heart. Dan grinned.

"Found you," he said aloud to the screen. Dan looked at the author of the article and opened another window. He typed in the details of the murder and hit Enter. As he waited for the computer to find the information, he called the reporter.

"Kelso, how are you?" Dan asked when the phone was answered. "Good. What exactly do you want?" Kelso asked.

"Some information," Dan answered.

"You know damn well I can't give up my sources, Dan, so quit asking."

"What if I told you I had information on a possible serial killer?" Dan asked quietly. Kelso stayed quiet. Dan could hear the television in the background.

"I'd need the information first before I told you who my sources were—" Dan cut Kelso off.

"No, it doesn't work like that, Kelso. If you want me to tell you what I know, then you need to give me something." Dan waited for him to reply. He could almost hear him arguing with himself. Finally he sighed.

"OK, what do you want to know?" Kelso asked.

"Did you read the article on the girl that was found in the marshlands?" he asked.

"Yeah, what about it?" Kelso asked.

"Who gave you the evidence material?" Dan asked.

"Your information had better be bloody good, Dan, that source took a long time to work and is worth a shitload," Kelso warned. Dan stayed silent, waiting for Kelso to give whoever it was up.

"Fine, it's a detective in the Henderson station. She works forensics. Now, what have you got for me, and it better be good." Dan thought how he could word his response without giving anything away.

"Many of the homicides within the last year may have a link to them," Dan stated. Silence filled the line. Kelso took a breath as if he meant to ask a question, but Dan cut him off quickly.

"If you dig a bit deeper, you might be able to find something useful, Kelso." Dan killed the line, turned the phone off, and shoved it in his pocket. He knew that Kelso would be fuming over that little stunt, but the guy was a sucker for a good story, and he knew where he would go if anything newsworthy happened.

Dan typed into the search engine "Female Detective Henderson Police station" and hit Enter. A few talented keystrokes later, the screen redrew with the police stations intranet. He navigated to the pages that listed the officers and information about them and found the person he was looking for.

"Megan Webb." Dan pulled his cell phone out again and powered it up. The phone bleeped impatiently at him, indicating that he had four missed calls—in the space of three minutes. All of them from Kelso. He ignored them and pressed in the number for the direct line to Megan's desk. A recorded message began playing after the third ring. He left a suitably cryptic message then hung up the phone. What now he thought.

What was he supposed to do here that he couldn't be doing at home? Mr. Vigilante was probably annoyed he'd been noticed, and judging by some of his (possible) previous work, he wasn't the kind of guy you'd want to piss off. On the other hand, maybe Mr. Vigilante might want help acquiring some of that hard-to-reach information. After all, he's only taking out the bad guys, right? Dan looked off into the darkness. Anybody could be there watching him. Shaking it off, he tapped the mouse and brought up a search engine again, and this time looked for her in the online phone directory. "Bingo. That was almost too easy."

A small scuffing sound echoed behind him and he spun around abruptly. Nothing but more darkness looked back at him. Slowly, he turned back to the screen and looked at the address. He wrote it down on the back of his hand. Got a good look at the area with satellite pictures. Closed the computer and stood up. He left the computer where it had been found and walked back outside into the cold night.

I watched from the darkness. So far he hadn't shown me anything that was overly spectacular. It had taken us both roughly the same amount of time to find the detective's name and her home address, which, in my opinion, left her horribly exposed. I watched Dan walk out of the building and climb over the fence and into his car.

After he was gone, I waited another five minutes without moving then gave it another minute. Slowly I walked out of the shadows and over to the laptop. I pulled a can of lighter fluid from my pocket and poured it all over its top. The light from my Zippo was painfully bright. The flame touched the edge of the computer then spread violently across the top as I turned and walked off into the night. By the time I had climbed over the fence, the computer was completely engulfed in flames.

CHAPTER 17

"Jakob! Please pay attention!" the teacher called. "If you don't pay attention, Jakob, you can stand in the corner! Again." Her stare was menacing while she yelled.

The rest of the class turned to stare at him as well. Jakob could feel his face turning red. He looked at the floor and kept silent until the teacher began reading from the book again. It was only then that he chanced a look up, seeing all the rest of the children sitting on the floor with him. Most were paying attention to the teacher, all except for two girls sitting directly across from him. Two girls with honey blonde hair and bright blue eyes, Michelle and Kelly.

He watched them cast sideways glances at him and whisper to each other. These two were the adults' darlings, beautiful, smart, but he wasn't the only kid in school who'd seen an uglier, vicious side. He just knew they were talking about him, but he couldn't do anything about it.

Jakob walked slowly into the vast hallway. Down one side, it had thirty hooks screwed to the wall. Every single one of them had a bag hung on it next to a rain coat. His was in the middle. This was part of the day he hated the most. It was the most opportune time for the other children to pick on him. He pulled an apple out of his bag and took a small bite. His unruly shock of blond hair fell over the front of his face, partially covering is eyes. "You know, Jakob, you really should do as you are told," a girl's bright young voice said from behind him. Jakob froze mid bite. He leaned forward unconsciously trying to get as far away from her as he possibly could. He looked up and down the hallway and couldn't see anybody, which meant bad news for him. Slowly, he turned around and started to walk away but was stopped by a hand on his chest. Jakob looked down at it then followed its arm, eventually settling on Kelly's dazzlingly blue eyes. She was a year older, angelic, and he knew he was in trouble the moment he looked at her. "It's not polite to disrupt the class, especially when the teacher is talking. Even if you really are nothing, you could at least try to behave like us civilised people," she said with a completely straight face pointing at Michelle and herself.

Michelle joined Kelly, stepping in front of him, to block his path to the door at the end of the hallway.

"You know, we may just let you go. If you do something for us," Michelle taunted. Jakob really didn't want to answer; he just wanted to get out of there and back to the classroom. He looked past her towards the door and to what he was sure was freedom. Kelly's fist bunched around the front of his shirt and pulled him in close. His chest was pushing up against hers, and he could feel one of her legs pressing against the front of his. Michelle pressed her full length from behind him, squashing him in between the two. The tall blonde leaned in close, so her lips were next to his ear. He could smell her freshly washed hair. It smelt sweet, like strawberries.

"You are going to meet us down by the river today after school for a special treat. Something we've both wanted to try with a boy." She comically batted her eyes at him. "You will turn up for us, or I will make sure you regret it," she whispered. Kelly let go of Jakob's shirt, and they both stepped away in unison just as the principal emerged from the classroom. He looked down the hallway towards them, locking eyes with Jakob. Looking away quickly, Jakob put his head down and walked for the door that led outside onto the playing field. He had to get away from them.

Jakob walked down the road away from school and towards home. It was a bright summer's day, and it was nearing the end of term. He couldn't wait for school to finish. Jakob much preferred to be at home sitting on their old brown vinyl couch, watching Saturday morning cartoons.

Jakob trudged up a small rise in the road. He had argued with himself all day as to whether he should go to the river like the mean girls had told him. His initial reaction was to run. But then he thought about it more carefully. He was curious, but the thought of being beaten up by two girls scared him away. There was definitely something naughty going on with these girls, and they were so very pretty. Maybe these two cute girls had picked him to share in their naughtiness for a good reason, and they weren't going to hurt him. He'd be "the man" then. A pinprick of hope poked through the fear.

He slowly crested the rise in the road and looked to his left. In the shallow gully below, he could see the river snaking its way towards the school. It meandered its way towards the line of trees that bordered the playing field then doglegged to the right and made its way around the edge. Jakob could see the other side of the river but not the side closest to him. He stepped up to the fence running alongside the road and peered over it. Down near the bank, hidden by the hillside and out of view of the road, stood the two girls. They stood there next to each other, looking up the small bank directly at Jakob. He felt his heart skip a beat.

"You do remember our deal, Jakob? You help us try something with a boy, and we leave you alone. Run away and you'll regret it—do you hear?" He looked down at them then turned back down the road towards home. Returning his gaze back down to the bank, the girls had already disappeared from view. He couldn't see them anywhere, and that scared him. He turned and began to walk along the side of the road again, hoping he would be able to get away from the two of them.

"Didn't I say that you would regret it if you didn't come down to the river with us. Jakob? It's not nice to keep a girl waiting, especially if they like you." Jakob stopped and turned around quickly but saw no one behind him. He turned back, and one of the girls stepped out of the long grass. She was standing a few feet in front of him and smiling like a model in one of those fashion ads. Jakob could not help but smiling back. A hand clamped down on his shoulder from behind him and pushed him towards the fence. "You're coming with us, Jakob," the girl behind him said. They pushed him down the bank towards the river, the road disappearing from view.

Kelly and Michelle stood either side of him, with Jakob facing the river; he could hear the splash and flow of the deep water as it moved between the banks. Although strangely excited, he was also frightened and desperately wanting to go home. The young boy knew his parents would be angry if he arrived home late. He didn't want to stay.

Jakob felt a hand rest gently on his shoulder. It turned him to face the quieter of the two. As he looked up into her shimmering blue eyes, she smiled. Her perfect white teeth were like gleaming pearls between her lips. Jakob was awestruck and smiled back, then a brief moment later, realised how stupid he probably looked.

A hand reached around from behind and grabbed his shorts. Before he could protest, his shorts were dragged down around his ankles, taking his underpants with them and revealing him to the girls. They took a half a step backwards and giggled. Jakob was rooted to the spot; he couldn't move. His eyes bugged from his head as his mind refused to believe what was happening. He reached down to pull his pants up but was met with a vicious blow to the side of his head with a leather shoe. Jakob's eyes rolled into the back of their sockets, and he fell to the ground.

"Wake up, Jakob, wake up!" a voice told him. It sounded like it was hovering near the edge of his consciousness, and he wasn't quite solid enough to reach it. Jakob groaned and breathed in deeply, the scent of fresh grass filling his lungs. Then something else, something different. Something that smelt sweet but with a sharp edge. Jakob opened his eyes but couldn't see anything. He could only see the faintest hint of light. He tried to move but found it was impossible. Panic closed in and gripped his heart like a vice. He struggled and thrashed but could barely move. A hand clamped around his throat, and he stopped moving, struggling to breathe. Jakob tried to sit up and felt an unbearable stinging between his legs. He tried to scream, but before the sound could escape, something hard and unforgiving was pushed firmly into his mouth.

An hour rolled past as if it were a year. They touched him everywhere. He was sore all over, but they paid particular attention to what they found between his legs. He began to itch all over, and he tried to raise his hands to scratch it. Jakob cried and struggled until he grew tired, then he gave up, just laying still and waiting for it to end.

The end came abruptly. The blindfold was removed, and he screwed his eyes shut, the sunlight blinding him. Slowly he opened his eyes, and the image in front of him swam into focus. Kelly and Michelle stood side by side, holding hands. They were naked. Jakob took in their milky white skin as his eyes moved up their long slender thighs. He settled on their chests and couldn't believe what he was seeing.

"Do you like what you see, Jakob? Or do you prefer boys?" Kelly asked. Jakob struggled to move. Michelle bent down in front of Jakob and yanked the hard object from his mouth so he could answer her.

"Well, do you like what you see, or do you prefer little boys?" she asked again. He stayed quiet but kept his eyes on the pair. He was too tired to fight, but to say something now could make it worse. One turned to the other, and they looked at each other questioningly.

"I guess no answer means he doesn't like us. This means he likes boys instead." They both looked down at him in disgust.

"I guess that means he wants something else we don't have. But we can give him the experience," Kelly said sweetly. She turned and walked away towards the river bank. Jakob watched as she bent down and picked up a stick the size of her wrist. She turned with a wicked grin on her face and walked slowly back towards him. Terror ripped through him when he realised what the two girls were going to do. He didn't care what they thought of him now, crying and sniffling. He struggled and thrashed violently but couldn't move. A foot kicked at him hard, pushing him onto his stomach, and then pressed hard down on the back of his neck. He began to scream when he realised there was no escape.

Chapter 18

Megan sat in front of her computer at her desk. It was ten at night, and she was working late. Both of the two cases she had on the go were beginning to get to her. So far they had no leads. The name Norman Octavia had led her down a dead end, as she guessed it would. The address he had supplied was for a vacant lot, which left her with nowhere else to turn. She had a sketch artist draw an interpretation of him, but she thought he was almost certainly disguised. Some basics such as height and frame were about all she could count on.

Megan reread the details of the two murders. Another thing, she still didn't know was if the two were connected. Other than the victim profile, there was not a lot else to connect them. It irritated her no end that she couldn't get a bead on the perp. No common start points on the cases, no common methods. She looked at the crime scene photos again, her stomach reacting almost as strongly as the first time she had seen them. First the set from the little girl found in the marsh, and then the girl found in the dumpster. She studied the photos of the dumpster girl; in particular, she paid even closer attention to the cuts on her torso. They were deep, but not as deep as she had originally thought. They had already identified that they were likely made with a shard of glass, as small fragments had been left behind. The killer was indiscriminate and random as to where he positioned them. He/she had not planned these cuts, probably succumbing to a blind rage. She had also discerned that the killer was right-handed and fairly tall, probably at least six feet.

She studied the photos of the little girl. She ground her teeth together when she saw the rope burns around her neck. The rope had been there longer than a few minutes, and this girl had suffered. Megan's line of work was never pretty, but she couldn't stand it when a child was harmed. Whoever did this deserved whatever justice was handed out to him—and then some.

Megan picked up the autopsy report and read through it again slowly. It was very sparse and factual. The examiner had determined the cause of death to be by strangulation. There were large bruises on her arms and back, but nothing seemed to have been inflicted post-mortem. There was a small scar on the inside of her left thigh, but the healed skin indicated that it had nothing to do with the case. She picked up the photos of the crime scene and examined them all over again. She didn't want to miss even the smallest clue.

It was getting late; Megan turned off her desk lamp and the office plunged into a dull darkness. The furniture formed dark shadows, illuminated only by the street lights from outside the station. She shut down her computer and walked out the front door. If only the work was just as easily shut off.

She could feel her eyelids drooping heavily as she drove the short distance to her home. Her gun dug uncomfortably into her back as she negotiated the various roundabouts in the road, the periodic discomfort was just enough to keep her awake. Megan pulled into her short driveway and climbed out into the cool night air. The door slammed shut and was locked before she headed up the garden path to the front door. Megan dug into her handbag to remove her house keys as she stepped onto the landing in the darkness. She froze. The door hung open by the smallest margin. She stood still, peering into the darkness of her hallway. As silently as she could, she slipped her keys into her bag and placed it on the landing next to the door. Her hand snaked to her back, and she drew her pistol, silently slipping a round into the chamber as she did so. Her heart began to thump wildly as she pushed the door slowly open. She stood there, looking into the gloom and listening for any sign of someone who shouldn't be there, however minute. Stepping into the darkness, she gently closed the door behind her then stood quietly listening. Megan moved slowly into the hallway towards the kitchen at the end of the hallway. She had one slim advantage; this was her house, and she knew her way around in the dark. The backdoor led out into the rear yard, but it was small and offered no ready escape. She brought the gun to bear and moved towards the open doorway at the end of the hall. She stepped through it and swung to her right, then back to her left to look into the lounge area. At the opposite end of the lounge was a set of stairs leading up to the master bedroom. She moved silently across the carpet towards them and stopped.

A distinct knock from up the stairwell made her heart skip a beat, and adrenaline surged into her veins. She placed her left foot onto the lower step and began ascending the stairs towards her room.

It all happened so fast, she didn't have time to aim her shot. A figure at the top of the stairs appeared and began running towards her taking the steps three at a time. This person hit her front on, pushing her back onto the floor and knocking the wind from her lungs. Hastily, she pulled the trigger, the crashing sound in the confined space causing her ears to ring. The flash from the muzzle lit the area around her. She saw a large person moving rapidly towards the kitchen. Megan rolled onto her stomach and yanked the trigger again.

Breathing heavily, she stood up and stalked quickly towards the front door. It hung open, and the street was empty. Megan searched the rest of the house but could not find anything.

"Are you all right?" Holmes asked her again, as uniformed officers searched her place. Megan nodded.

"We need to lock this place down. It's a crime scene until we can clear it." Holmes stated. "Go and get some clothes together and we will get you someplace safe tonight." Megan was about to protest when an officer come thudding down the stairs to stand in front of them.

"Uh. Sir? I think you better come take a look at this." Holmes looked at him with a puzzled expression then followed the rather grim-looking officer up the stairs. They moved quickly into her bedroom, where whatever had affected him seemed to be. A ring of photos had been assembled around the walls of the room at eye level. Megan walked up to one of the nearest ones and looked closely at it. She turned away, her face ashen.

"Oh my god," Holmes breathed, wandering around the room. "What kind of sicko are we dealing with here?" No one answered.

The photos showed girls in varying states. Some were completely mutilated, some were still alive. The photos were dulling with age at the start of the ring and progressively getting newer until they ended abruptly. Megan looked at the last photo in the sequence. It was the girl from the dumpster. Three of the photos showed her kneeling in a steel cage barely big enough for her to stand up in. Megan studied it closely; the girl had her eyes closed and her head bowed.

"Her name was Anna," Megan whispered. "Excuse me?" Holmes asked.

"The body we found in the dumpster, her name was Anna." Megan stepped back and looked carefully around her room. Her gaze settled on her chest of drawers sitting in the corner near the wardrobe. Something looked wrong. She looked at the top draw carefully and instantly felt repulsed. It had been opened. The search team had only just walked into this room, so it hadn't yet been touched by them. She walked slowly past the captain towards the drawer and carefully pulled it open with gloved hands. It was empty, totally bare. Megan turned away and looked at Holmes.

"What is it?" he asked.

Megan said nothing; she headed for the door and ran down the stairs. She had to get outside and away from here, her home; it had been violated, and as far as she was concerned, she didn't live there anymore.

Chapter 19

I pushed the power button on the remote, and the television flickered to life. I sat down in the single-seater and changed it to the current affairs channel. I was just in time to catch a bulletin on the body found in the city dumpster. Although billed as a live transmission, it was pretty obvious that it had been recorded earlier in the day. I could see the Envirowaste truck still jammed down a narrow alleyway behind the reporter who stood and looked forlornly into the camera lens.

"Another body has been uncovered in the early hours of this morning by a council employee. His name has been suppressed while he speaks to the police, but it doesn't appear as though they are pressing any charges. At this early stage, it is believed that the employee has nothing to do with the grisly scene found here." The reporter turned and indicated towards the truck, before turning her pretty face back to the camera.

I sighed; that meant they didn't have anyone that was worth looking at yet. In fact they probably had shit to go on "at this early stage." Which meant the sick fuck that pulled this little stunt was still out there, probably getting ready to do it again. I looked at my laptop just as the chime sounded telling me an e-mail had arrived.

Have you been watching? I frowned then looked at the user name. JR44.

I placed my hands on the keyboard then paused.

I have no idea what you are talking about. I typed then hit Enter. I waited for JR44 to reply.

You should. It's all over the news right now. I know you know about my little swamp flower too. Whilst the public are all suitably horrified, they didn't know how disobedient she was. If the little bitch had just shut her trap, she wouldn't be where I left her.

I winced, looked at the television screen, then back at the computer screen. I minimised the chat programme and started a locator program a previous colleague had written. If he was in New Zealand, then this would pinpoint his location. It hadn't let me down yet.

The program started and asked me what I wanted to find. I gave it a few relevant bits of information, including the user name, and hit the Start button. I moved the mouse and brought the chat screen back up. A message waited for me.

Ha! You'll never find me; that antiquated program you're using is so far out of date it couldn't catch a virus. Although I don't want attention from either you or her, you are more than welcome to try.

Who was *her?* I sat back in my chair and shook my head. He was a sick bastard, but so far, pretty smart. Someone I'd like to get to before the cops did. My type of justice was what the people wanted, but were too afraid to say out loud. Any of the remaining public figures that publicly supported the death penalty soon found themselves handing in their resignation.

I ignored the obvious taunt and picked up the phone. I dialled a number from memory.

"Yeah?" the sleepy voice asked.

"Dan, if you were good enough, you should have found me by now."

"I have. You live in the city. Number 40 Leslie Avenue to be exact."

I grinned; he had found the address my computer whiz of a friend in Wellington had left for him.

"OK, I have a user name I want you to find. You got a pen?" I asked. "OK, shoot."

"The mongrel I'm looking for is calling himself JR44." I propped the phone against my shoulder while I poured myself a glass of water.

"Mongrel? Sounds as though you don't like this guy much. OK, this JR44—what does that mean?" he asked.

On my end of the line, I rolled my eyes. "I don't know. That's why you are going to find him for me." I was again doubting my decision to involve this guy.

'OK, I'll see what I can do."

The line went dead, and I dropped the handset back into the cradle. I looked back at the computer screen. Another message was flashing for my attention.

I'm going to do this again, Spangle36. I am going to continue until I get the respect I deserve. There is nothing you can do to stop me. I read the message again and slammed the screen shut. "Not if I get my hands around your neck first, you asshole," I mumbled.

I shut off the lights and walked down the short hallway to the bedroom. I fell into the bed, shucking off my shoes as I did so. Pulling a blanket over top of my clothes, I shut my eyes then quickly drifted off into a restless sleep.

CHAPTER 20

Jakob walked to school a week later. He had managed to convince his mother that he was sick and needed to stay home. He was still in some pain and could still feel the sting from the stick the two girls had used. Not letting his mother know had been the hardest part. He walked slowly, carefully down the short rural road and past the fence that hid the bank by the river. His eyes stayed glued to the dirt footpath; he didn't look up once. Jakob walked onto the school grounds like a slow-moving robot. He was late again and knew he was going to get punished for it.

But school detention was the least of his cares; he had other things on his mind—there were other things that required his attention. Jakob uncomfortably climbed the short stairs of the building and walked slowly towards the door that led to the classrooms. The school was old; his parents had attended here, which, in his mind, made it ancient. He walked past the first classroom to the next, where the older kids were settling down for the first lesson of the day.

Jakob pushed the door open reluctantly and trudged in.

"Would you please explain why you are late today, Jakob? I have a note excusing you for the past few days, but now that you're back, I expect you to be on time," said the teacher, in her usual way.

Jakob walked around to his desk at the back of the room and dropped his bag on the floor. It landed with a heavy thump. He scraped his chair back and dropped himself in it, ignoring the teacher altogether.

"Jakob Richardson, I asked you a question. Do not make me ask it again." The teacher raised her voice. Jakob ignored her and stared at the board at the far end of the classroom.

"Principal's office. Now." The woman pointed at the door.

Jakob swung his dull eyes at the teacher then at the door and began to laugh. It was a nasal cackle that echoed through the room. He stood up slowly and walked towards the door. His laughter died slowly as he disappeared down the long hallway towards the dreaded principal's office. He dropped himself into the seat outside the office door and waited quietly, the leftovers of a disbelieving smile still on his lips.

It took the teacher half an hour to leave the classroom and walk towards him. Jakob kept his eyes on her all the way to the door. He began to hear a little voice in his head. At first he couldn't understand what it was saying and ignored it. The door swung open, and the principal stuck her head into the hallway.

"Jakob," she said, indicating for him to come in. She then disappeared back inside leaving the door open. Jakob stood up slowly and walked into the office, carelessly slamming the door shut behind him.

CHAPTER 21

T he New Year came and went for Jakob. To him it was just another day. He was starting his final year in high school and looked forward of being rid of the place. He hated it in Matamata. His parents had shipped him off to boarding school thinking that it would change his behaviour. It didn't and never would. He did enough to get by and learn what he could, but other than that, he wanted nothing more than to leave. Jakob walked onto campus, late as usual, but he was pretty sure the teachers had stopped caring. He was one that was going to fall through the cracks of the education system. He didn't care though; he already had his life mapped out, all in great detail. He was headed for the armed forces, come hell or high water. Gently he pushed open the fire doors into the corridor and walked quietly towards his first class. Well, technically if he had arrived on time, it would have been his third class, but he had something more urgent that morning which had required his attention. He pushed the door open and walked in. The teacher stopped to look at him.

"Mr. Richardson, that's the third time this week you have been this late. You're already on probation. If it happens again, I'm going to have to recommend that you be expelled," the English teacher said sternly.

Jakob ignored him and planted himself down in a free seat. He had already done all he needed to get into the army, and anything else didn't matter to him.

Silence filled the room as the teacher waited for any response. When he realised that none was forthcoming, he turned back to the rest of the class and continued on with the lesson.

Jakob didn't bother getting his books out; it was the next class he was interested in. He was trying his level best to get kicked out of English, but no matter what he did, the teacher, Axle Harvey, would not cave in to it. So he decided to go that little bit extra. He had stopped at a local dairy on the way to school and brought a pornographic magazine. It was still in its clear wrapper.

He didn't really care for that type of magazine; in fact, he detested them. He hated woman with more passion than he wanted to live, especially the pretty two-faced ones. He ignored any girl that approached him, which made all sorts of rumours spread like wildfire. He largely ignored any taunts because he knew he was above them in every way.

The bell reverberated around the buildings and the class disappeared faster than normal.

"Mr. Richardson, would you stay behind please," the older man asked just as Jakob was about to stand up to leave. He stood still and waited until the last student had walked out of the classroom. The teacher walked around the desk and sat on its edge and stared at Jakob.

Jakob watched him carefully. He knew what was coming and welcomed it. He didn't want to be there, and the teachers all knew it.

"What's wrong, Jakob? Why are you so anti-school?" the teacher asked as he crossed his arms. Jakob stayed quiet, but in his mind, he was running through the many reasons he hated the place so much. He had become good at keeping to himself. He ignored the teacher and looked at the grey tiles in front of him.

"Jakob, if you keep this up, you won't be able to get a job anywhere. I doubt the army would even take you." The last comment made Jakob look up at him. Jakob stood up abruptly, knocking over the desk in front of him and he rushed at the teacher.

"Don't tell me what I can and cannot do, sir." He jabbed his finger into the teacher's chest to make his point and stormed out of the class. He headed outside, stopping to look across the crowded lunch area. Moving slowly among the students busy sitting, eating their lunch, most paid him no attention. Most were use to his queer antics; others were discreet enough with their stares so as not to attract his attention. But they didn't have to worry; it was not them he was interested in.

"Where the fuck are you two bitches." he mumbled to himself. He knew they were there, part of the "in" crowd, part of those who thought themselves elite and above the general country scum that surrounded them. He couldn't see them anywhere, and that irritated him no end. He glanced over at the common room held exclusively for the senior students. To his relief, he could see them sitting in one of the bay windows, talking to a large group of hangers-on. He felt the hatred swell at just the sight of them. After confirming their location, Jakob turned and walked slowly and deliberately towards the next class. He didn't want to be late for Anatomy.

Chapter 22

Megan stepped into the shower. It was two in the morning when she finally crawled into the hotel bed. It wasn't the best, but it was a damn sight better than sleeping in the bed that had been violated by that creep. Megan closed her eyes and saw the scene play over and over in her mind. She walked into her home and towards the stairs. Her next memory was the colossal noise of her pistol as she pulled the trigger. She wanted to find the asshole that had invaded her life and put him in the ground. She remembered looking at her chest of drawers in the corner of the room. Her stomach twisted into knots, and she leaned over the edge of the bed to dry retch.

Her dreams were filled with monsters and faceless men all hunting her. Powerless, she could do nothing to stop them. She ran, but something kept tearing at her skin, kept pulling her back. Megan ran, screaming into the darkness. She had to get away from this place no matter what the consequence. It didn't matter that she was naked, didn't matter that she was cut and bleeding, just as long as she escaped, somehow.

Megan awoke in a cold sweat, a scream fighting to escape her throat. She threw the covers back and ran for the small bathroom. She tripped against a chair leg and fell to the floor, slamming her head against the cold linoleum, almost knocking her out. She lifted her spinning head and tasted a mouthful of blood. Megan spat it out on the floor and lifted herself onto her elbows. She glanced at the door and lowered her head into her hands.

"Megan, you shouldn't be in here today. After that kind of experience, you should be somewhere else," Captain Holmes said as he walked into her office. Megan looked up from her laptop and straight into his eyes.

"It's OK. I need to find him and bring him in," she stated. Holmes looked at her for a second more, shook his head, then left, closing the door behind him.

Megan looked back at her computer screen. She was on a Web site the police regularly watched, one that they knew people used, people of interest to them. She had created a new user account and had every intention of deleting it after she was finished. Her user name was F0reign. She typed in her message and entered it on the board for everyone to read, and hoped he would be watching.

Megan deleted any trace of her message and closed her laptop then stood up. She shoved her chair back against the wall and walked to the door. Screw this. She pulled the door open and strode the few steps to Holmes's office.

"Captain? On second thought, I think I will leave after all."

Holmes looked at her for a second then walked towards her and put his arm around her. Her body flexed and went rigid. "Sure. Take as much time as you need," he said in a soft voice.

Megan pulled away, strode through the door, and out into the cold sunshine wondering what had just happened. She climbed into her car and left the parking lot in a hurry.

Holmes watched her leave. He was worried about her. Not so much about her safety, but more if she went and did something reckless. Holmes turned to a uniformed sergeant at the desk.

"Put a car after her, would you? And make sure she doesn't do something stupid." The sergeant nodded and lifted the phone.

Megan drove the short distance to her house. She stepped out of the car and scanned the surrounding area. Even though it was midmorning, she still felt horribly exposed. She walked slowly towards the front door and pushed the key into the slot. The door swung open then she stepped inside. As she stepped into the apartment, she realised she was holding her breath and let it out. Walking slowly down the length of the hallway, she tentatively placed her hands on the wall as she approached the kitchen. She edged into the lounge area and looked at the floor below the stairwell.

Megan lay down on the floor in the position she remembered being in. Quickly she drew her pistol then rolled over, aiming it in roughly the same place she had when she had pulled the trigger. She picked out the spot on the wall where the muzzle was pointing.

Megan stood up and walked slowly towards the far wall of the kitchen. At chest height, there was a hole in the wall and another lower down and closer to the entrance to the hallway. She knelt down on the carpet and looked carefully. She doubted she would find anything of use.

Slowly she stood up and walked towards the stairwell. She began to feel physically sick as she climbed the stairs to her bedroom. A few deep breaths later, she carefully pushed the door open and stepped in. The photos had been removed from the walls; they had been taken away as evidence. She walked slowly towards the chest of drawers again and pulled the top open a fraction to look in at the empty space. Megan slammed it shut and ran downstairs. She couldn't breathe the air in here and had to get out. Running outside, she stumbled and landed heavily on the pavement and started sobbing. Not bothering to pull herself up, she let her head fall to the ground.

CHAPTER 23

The alarm clock woke me at six in the morning. My hand flew out of bed and slammed the clock against the wall.

"Fuck off," I groan. I was in no mood for anything today. A dark cloud had settled over me last night, and now it looked like rain. I tore the covers off and staggered towards the shower. I turned the shower on until it was almost too hot to stand, and stepped into the stream. I thought about the last thing JR44 wrote, and my blood began to boil again. It had occurred to me sometime during the night that he may have had been referring to a cop on the case when he spoke of not wanting "her" attention.

Stepping out of the shower, I wrapped a towel around my waist. Today I needed to find this cop and see if she could give me any information about JR44 or the murders he claimed he was responsible for. I flicked on my laptop and sat down in front of it, water pooling at my feet. The screen flicked to life, but all I could do was glare at it blankly. The sun was on the rise, and my stomach was starting to churn. Giving up on the computer for now, I stood up, got dressed, and went to find something for breakfast.

It was ten o'clock in the morning before I headed for the door. I pulled the lock back, and the laptop beeped at me for the second time that morning. I turned and walked back towards it. My finger hit the space bar and the screen refreshed my e-mail account. There's a new e-mail with an unrecognisable user name, but I do recognise something else. The subject line has the word *Toys* written in it. It's from the message board.

I clicked on the link as I sat down in the seat and waited for the computer and the server to shake hands and get talking. I scrolled through the messages and found the one I was looking for. I moved the cursor to the hyperlink on the name and clicked it.

We need to meet, Logos coffee shop on Ponsonby road. Twelve o'clock.

I looked at the time at the bottom of the screen. Ten twenty. It would take me an hour just to get to the city. I pushed the screen down and headed for the door.

Traffic was jammed as usual. The roads built in the nineteen fifties aren't designed to handle the excessive amount of vehicles travelling on it now. Two lanes are just not enough. I finally arrived at the K road end of Ponsonby road. The road was jammed with cars and people all trying to look important in the eyes of other people. I parked in a space that had been kindly carved in half by another car and got out onto the sidewalk.

I hate places like this. People everywhere, doing what they have to do to get by. A shudder ran up my spine as I turned and, in every direction, saw only people and shops, people standing in front of them, people going into them and leaving them. I put my head down and walked swiftly down the street towards the address that had been left on the message board. The further I walked down Ponsonby road, the more the population of the sidewalk seemed to swell. I finally arrived at the coffee shop, five minutes late. Not my fault, but it still got on my nerves.

I'd be going into this meeting blind. I didn't know who I was supposed to meet or what they looked like. I was hoping like hell that it was JR44, but I knew that was wishful thinking. The guy may be twisted to hell, but I didn't think he was stupid, not for a single second. He had eluded police for this long. But then again, so had I. It was just that nobody had really tried to stop me. I was doing this world a favour.

I stepped into the busy café and scanned the tables looking for an empty one. No such luck. I walked towards the till at the far end of the shop and browsed the food for sale. I sneered in disgust. Ten dollars for a club sandwich was as close to highway robbery as one could get without actually pulling a gun on you.

I turned away as a line began to form behind me and pretended to look towards the street again. Out of the corner of my eye, I could see a young lady looking straight at me with a newspaper lying on the table in front of her. She was tall even though she was sitting down, and I could tell she was the athletic type. Her straight brown hair was cut just off her shoulders. I chanced a fleeting look at her and she held my gaze, her green eyes asking me the question if I'm the one she is looking for. I turned and walked towards an empty seat on the opposite side of her table. I stopped short with my hand resting on the back of the seat.

"Is this seat taken?"

The woman gestured at it but didn't say a word. I carefully pulled it away from the table, making sure not to hit any of the patrons who were jammed in like sardines next to me. She scrutinised me as I sat down, and before I had a chance to say anything, a waitress slipped through the crowd towards us.

"May I take your order please?" she asked.

I looked at her then asked for a herbal tea. The waitress looked at the cup in front of the woman on the other side of the table and didn't bother asking if she wanted a refill. She dodged her way back to the counter.

I waited a moment, drawing a lazy circle on the table top with my finger. I looked out the tops of my eyes and saw she was staring straight at me again.

"You want to say something? Otherwise I'm going."

She leaned forward across the table. "Are you Spangle36?" She had an accent. Couldn't pick it with just those few words.

I didn't immediately reply; just cast my eyes around the perimeter of the shop. No one stood out.

"There is something I need you to take care of for me," she said. "This isn't the most practical place to discuss work arrangements, lady.

Meet me on the street in ten minutes." I stood up to leave. I threw a couple dollars on the table for the tea I wasn't going to drink and started moving through the lunchtime crowd to the door. I looked up and down Ponsonby Road to see if anything obviously wrong jumped out at me, but it looked clear.

I walked to a nearby bus stop and sat down in the sunshine to wait. A bus pulled up to the curb, and the door swung open. The driver looked at me, and I shook my head once. The bus sped off in a cloud of diesel smoke and noise.

"He came into my home," she said as she sat down next to me. "You probably know who I am, so I'll get straight to the point."

I turned to look at her. "Before you go any further, do you know anything about bulletin boards they have in chat rooms?"

She nodded. "Yes."

"So you aren't JR44, are you?" I asked casually.

She shook her head. "No. My name is Megan Webb. I'm a police forensics detective. I use chat rooms regularly to monitor certain people that are of interest to the police."

I nodded in return. Standard response to a standard description, well- rehearsed, no doubt.

"That's how I found you," she continued.

I looked sideways at her. "I guess I'm not covering my tracks well enough then."

Megan shook her head. "No, you are doing more than enough. It wasn't easy to find you, and to be honest, I'd rather not know who you are. You have a lot of silent support for your . . . ah, work. Although as part of my job, I have been detailing all the help you have been anonymously giving us."

The last comment caught me off guard. I wasn't expecting to have my life's work followed and applauded.

"Like I said, someone came into my house. They left a few items for me to look at, and they also took a few personal belongings of mine. Needless to say, the items they took make me think he has a problem."

"You think it's a he?" I asked.

Megan nodded. "I caught him inside, in my bedroom to be precise. He had pinned photos of all his trophies around the walls of my bedroom. The last photo is of the young woman recently found in the dumpster with her legs cut off."

I nodded; I had read the headlines about it and seen more on the news, but so far there hadn't been any more details released.

"He goes by JR44," I stated.

Megan looked at me, her jaw dropping open slightly.

I carried on. "Apparently he has a thing for me. He keeps sending me messages asking if I like the artwork he has produced. He asked if I liked his art he had prepared in the wetlands, he called it 'Winters Bloom'.'."

Megan dropped her head into her hands. "I'm working that case," she whispered.

Even I could see she'd been affected more than she should have as a cop. An uncomfortable silence settled while she pulled herself together again. Another bus pulled up to the bus stop and the doors swung open. We both ignored the driver, and the bus sped off again, the doors closing as it pulled away.

"I want you to find him and take care of him," Megan said as she looked across the street.

I looked at her again. "Isn't that a job for the police? I mean, what you are asking me to do isn't leg . . ."

Megan cut me off by raising her hand swiftly.

"Cut the bullshit, we both know you could get this done a lot faster than the police." Her accent was cutting through.

I nodded. "OK, let's assume for a moment that I say yes, what guarantee will I have that you won't arrest me after I find him?" I asked. It felt like I was in some straight-to-DVD cop movie to ask it, but it was a question that would make or break the deal.

"I can only tell you what I will and will not do. I won't be chasing anyone for the murder of the person who has ruined my life. As for the rest of the force, you can guarantee they will do their duty and come after you. Does that answer your question?"

I nodded and stood up. "OK, I'll be in touch." I turned and walked off down the street, leaving her alone on the bus stop bench.

CHAPTER 24

Jakob sat across the street in his rented minivan. He had tailed the cop to the busy street in Ponsonby. It had been a major problem trying to find a parking space in the overcrowded area. It was the perfect scene though. The sheer amount of people allowed him to blend in effortlessly, she had no idea that he was there. He had followed her into the coffee shop and watched her closely as she had taken her seat at the only empty table. He could feel himself hardening being this close to her. She'd be used to taking orders. He'd stood in the middle of the room with her back to him, almost close enough to reach out and touch her. He had taken a few deep breaths and calmed himself. He was here because it was out of the ordinary for her, and he wanted to find out why.

He'd ordered a latte and a strawberry muffin. He'd also asked for ice cream, but was told they didn't have any, which disappointed him. He had just finished his muffin and begun to wonder why she'd chosen here to have her rather morose coffee break when a tall man walked in and stood in almost the same place he had and looked around. Jakob avoided eye contact with the man but kept him in his vision out of the corner of his eyes. He was dressed in jeans and a dark coloured shirt with short sleeves even though it was still winter. The man walked towards the counter and pretended to browse the items for sale. Jakob scoffed; even he could see that he was faking.

"What kind of idiot is this?" he mumbled to himself. Jakob watched the man cast a look at his girl. Instantly he hated him. The cop gestured to the man in response to some question then he sat down across the table from her. Jakob was screaming inside. The thought of another man even looking at something he considered his was enough to make his temper ignite.

But Jakob remained still. Even though he'd wanted nothing more than to stand up and kill the guy who was flirting with his property, he had to stay in the shadows for a while longer. He could take it out on her two-timing body later. Jakob sipped his latte carefully and watched the pair talk briefly in hushed tones.

Suddenly the man stood up and walked for the door. Jakob put down his cup and considered his options. He stood up and followed the man out the door. The man had stopped and scanned the street. Jakob studied his watch and waited for the man to move. He walked towards a bus stop and sat down. Jakob had waited for a gap in the traffic and crossed the street to his minivan.

The man had just left and walked down the street without even looking back at the cop. Jakob watched him go then disappear into the crowd. He cast his gaze over at Megan. She was still sitting on the bus stop bench. He sat there watching for twenty minutes, mentally undressing her as cars whipped past in a frenzied, stop-start race. A bus pulled up, and he watched Megan climb aboard and disappear into the traffic. Jakob looked up the road in the opposite direction, the direction the man had walked.

He wanted to find out who he was and what exactly he wanted with his property.

CHAPTER 25

Six months earlier

Jakob sat alone in a bar. People danced all around him as the music thumped, but still he felt like the only person on the planet. He looked at his half-empty beer bottle, which he had paid an extortionately high price for, and wondered how the management could get away with it.

He was in a Christchurch bar on Manchester Street, right next to the seedy area of town. He had heard good things about it on the bulletin boards and in the chat rooms so he decided to check it out for himself. Music thumped and people danced all around him making his mood grow dimmer. He had tried to talk to a handful of people at the start of the night and had been told quite frankly and rudely to go away.

He spun on the seat and leaned back against the bar holding the bottle in one hand. He had been in many bars similar to this, and he knew how to play the game. He scanned the room for the biggest male he could find. Two tall guys, well over six feet, danced near the back of the club with five girls around them. He sat there watching as three songs started and finished, and he finished his beer. Jakob stood slowly and, casually, slipped the glass bottle into his back pocket. Adjusting his coat slightly, it draped over the bottle, hiding it well. Leaving, he walked outside and headed across the street. He stopped in the middle of the street to let a police car slip past, paying the occupants no attention. The side alley he slipped into was dark so he turned and leaned against the rough brick wall to wait.

Benjamin and Simon danced with the girls as the music battered their senses. They didn't care though; they had just won the pairs sculls at the Mardi Rowing Cup, beating out at least a dozen other schools for the coveted prize. They had also been in the winning crew for the eights. Simon could feel the beer; he knew he had too many in him and was going to pay severely for it in the morning, but at the moment, he didn't care—he was having fun. The pair had walked confidently into the loudest club they could find and were instantly converged on by girls and guys alike. They didn't mind being famous; both of them were virgins, but they were hoping their luck would change tonight.

Simon put his lips close to the ear of one of the blondes that was dancing with them.

"Shall we get out of here?" he yelled.

The girl turned to look at him with a puzzled look. Simon gestured to the door, and the girl smiled her acceptance. Simon caught Benjamin's eye, and the group began snaking its way through the crowd towards the door. The night air was cold, and Simon shivered as they stepped into the sidewalk. He looked up and down the street trying to decide in which direction they should go.

"I'm hungry," one of the girls complained.

"Sorted! Let's go that way then," Benjamin said as he jabbed a finger towards a restaurant area. The group began to walk off, soon splitting into two groups, the five girls out front with the two boys trailing behind.

The view was better back here anyway. Ben thought to himself.

"Hell, its cold out here tonight!" Simon shoved his hands deep into his pockets of his jeans as if to emphasise the point.

"Yeah, imagine how they must be feeling," Benjamin replied indicating in the direction of the girls in front of them. They wore miniskirts and tight-fitting tops. Leather platform boots or high heels were mandatory if you wanted to get noticed, bare legs on all of them. It didn't seem to matter that the temperature was almost freezing, as long as they looked good.

Benjamin leaned over to Simon as they turned down a shortcut between two buildings; the street at the opposite end cast a dull light down the bricked alleyway.

"I'm after the blonde," Benjamin whispered. Simon looked at him and said nothing in reply; he was interested in the brunette.

There was a squeal, and one of the girls fell over. In those boots, it was not surprising she'd twisted her ankle on the uneven surface of the cobbles. Simon and Benjamin both ran forward, grabbing her at the same time to help her to her feet. Simon looked over at Benjamin with a smirk on his face. He could see right down her top.

The girl was wobbling unsteadily on her feet, so they helped her to a seat bolted to a brick wall. The girl sat down heavily as the group gathered around them. The four girls knelt down in front of their friend and began whispering to each other. The guys took their cue and moved off down the street a short way out of earshot.

"Did you see that?" Simon asked as he spun around. Benjamin nodded in the darkness. Simon could only make out the faint motion of his head. "I think I'll change my mind and take her instead," Simon stated as he swung back around to look at the group. His back was to Benjamin.

Simon looked at the girls lustfully and began thinking about the night ahead. Then everything turned dull. Like someone turned out the lights. He tried to turn to Benjamin but found himself lying face down on the cobblestones forming the dark street. A figure stepped over him and walked down the street, away from them, towards the girls.

Sensing danger, Simon tried to get up. He couldn't feel his arms, and his legs wouldn't work. He began to panic. Unknown to him, the glass shard had slipped between the vertebrae of his spine, severing the spinal cord just below where the skull joins the neck.

The figure stepped close to the group of girls, and Simon thought he heard the person ask if they needed some help. The man bent down and scooped up the young girl and walked down the street with her in his arms. The group of girls followed and disappeared around the corner with the man.

Michaela opened the stainless steel fridge and removed a carton of orange juice. She grabbed a packet of bacon and cracked two eggs into a frying pan. She was getting breakfast ready for her son, Simon. She had promised him that today they would do whatever he liked. She knew he felt bad for not spending enough time with her, and she didn't mind it at all. At the moment, her son was a city-wide sporting icon in Christchurch and she was the proudest mother. She clicked on the small television set sitting on at the end of the bench close to the wall.

"In breaking news this morning, the body of nineteen-year-old Emma Jackson was found floating face down in the Avon River near Hagley Park earlier this morning. Police are treating the death as suspicious. Also two young males believed to be part of the Christchurch Boys College gold-medal-winning rowing team have been rushed to hospital in critical conditions. The two young boys were found on a suburban street in the early hours of the morning..."

A strangled noise came out of Michaela's throat. Her hand began to shake uncontrollably, and she dropped her cup to the floor. She didn't hear the knock at the door at first; she was locked to the TV screen. Another knock, louder this time, startled her, and she gave a short silly little laugh. She pulled herself together and straightened her robe and went to answer the door. Two police officers stood in the doorway in the dull light of the new morning. Michaela began to tremble again, her hand covering her mouth.

She collapsed to the floor, unconscious.

CHAPTER 26

Jakob sipped a beer as the jet rocked backwards and headed for the skies. He watched the shapely hostess walk past him and settle herself in the seats near the rear of the aircraft. He had deliberately asked for a seat this far back. He sipped his beer and poked his head out into the aisle, looking down the length of the aircraft. Leaning back into his chair he started to relax and closed his eyes to remember the fun he had last night with young Emma.

Her friends had totally bought his story. He was a trainee doctor interning at Dunedin hospital and was in Christchurch for the weekend. He told the group he knew some of the doctors at Christchurch hospital and that he would take her there to get her ankle attended to. The girls had complimented him on his selfless act and thanked him. They wanted to come along, but he told them that he only had a small car, and it was full of clothes and books.

Of course he looked completely different now. His long hair was gone, and the scar running from the corner of his left eye to the corner of his lip had disappeared. He wanted to be memorable, but he also wanted to be unrecognisable. He thought he had achieved that before he left the hotel room and headed for the airport.

He pulled on the headphones and flicked through the channels on the small monitor mounted in the seat in front of him. He turned to the news channel and listened to the report of the girl found floating face down in the Avon river.

"That was the easy part," he thought to himself. Jakob smiled as the thoughts and memories came flooding back. She had a sweet scent; she had tasted even sweeter. He remembered his fingers wrapped into the long golden locks of hair that fell around her shoulders. Blood from her wrists had sprayed a beautiful pattern, staining the tight shirt she was wearing.

Jakob had found an old house on the outskirts of Christchurch and had put it to good use. He didn't need much, only a length of rope and a few pulleys. Easily found at the local hardware store. He did bring one object with him in his small checked bag. To the average eye, it was a small, miniature baseball bat about a foot long. It wasn't much to look at, but Jakob, being the flawless craftsman, had designed something that would be devastating. With a twist of the handle, a series of razor blades imbedded in the thicker end flicked out around the circumference. The blades only sat away from the metal shell by a fraction, but that was all that was needed to make for the worst of pain.

Jakob tied Emma's hands behind her back then hoisted her off the cold dusty floor by her feet. Emma screamed into the cloth gag wedged in her mouth. The pain on her ankles was more than anything she had ever experienced. Jakob stood in front of her, the dull light from the kerosene lamp forming a dark silhouette. Emma saw him pull a knife from his pocket as he walked towards her. Emma screwed her eyes shut and began to scream again. She could feel his hands all over her as he cut away her clothing, leaving her naked, hanging by her ankles from the rafters above.

Blood rushed to her head, and she began to feel dizzy. She desperately wanted to go home, wanted to see her parents and her brother and sister again.

"Did you honestly think you could get away with it?" Jakob asked her.

Emma stopped struggling and began to wonder what this maniac was talking about.

"I saw you, across the dance floor. Flirting with that young weed you called a man. Using your body to get what you want." He bent down and spat in her face. Emma began to shake her head. She wasn't trying to do anything, she was only out for a good time with some friends. Jakob watched her shake her head violently from side to side.

"Do you think I'm stupid, Emma? Yes, that's right! I know all about you and your kind! That's all a woman uses her body for, is to flirt and fuck," he yelled. Jakob stood up slowly and moved into the shadows.

"Now that we know this we will be able to stop it, won't we, Emma." Emma struggled trying to twist around to see what the madman was going to do next. She caught a glimpse of something being pulled from a small bag, something metallic. Jakob turned away, and Emma lost sight of it. She started to beg and plead, but the dank cloth turned her voice into a muffled cry. Panic began to grip her. Her flesh crawled as her mind began to race through the horror that was coming.

"Look, I made this especially for you." Jakob bent down in front of Emma holding a tapered cylinder. It had a series of small slits running lengthwise for exactly half its length. Emma's confusion evaporated into a blood-freezing panic. Jakob flicked his wrist and a soft metallic sound echoed around the room. Razor blades sprang from the slits. He flicked his wrist the opposite direction and the blades retracted.

Jakob grinned as his captive began to thrash and scream, the rope cutting deeper into her ankles.

Jakob stood up and looked at her pelvis in the dull light. He was disgusted by the sight, and the feel of it only made him more determined to get rid of it. Jakob forced her legs apart with his left arm. He raised the metal cylinder between her knees and drove it deep inside her. Emma groaned as the cylinder forced her open. Her eyes rolled back as the pain began to increase the deeper he pushed.

Finally Jakob stopped, Emma, hanging by her ankles, remained still, her back arched in an almost unnatural position. Her breathing was rapid and shallow, her heart racing. Jakob bent down and looked Emma in the eyes. Tears dribbled down her forehead as she began to realise that there was no escaping.

"Do you think they will miss you, Emma? Do you think they will come looking for you?"

He stood up quickly and closed his fingers around the handle of the bat, and twisted, there was a soft click. Emma began to convulse. She vomited around the gag, causing Jakob to step back and to let go of the handle. He looked down at the mess on the floor and began to laugh. Jakob stepped forward and grabbed the handle in a tight grip.

"Good night, Emma, sweet dreams." He jerked his hand up ripping the tube from her. An arc of blood followed the blades staining the floor. Emma's spasms quickened and then she passed out.

Jakob watched blood flow in rivers down her stomach and drip from the end of her nose onto the floor.

"Excuse me, sir, we are about to land, would you mind folding the tray table up please?"

The hostess startled Jakob from his daydream. He lifted the table and latched it away then waited for the plane to touch down. He was eager to get back home so he could post some comments on the board.

Chapter 27

I pulled open the ranch slider and stepped inside, slamming it shut behind me. I knew this asshole JR44 was behind it. He was responsible for the young girl and the body in the dumpster. I sat down at my laptop again and picked up my phone.

"Have you found anything yet?" I asked when Dan answered.

"Yeah, at first it says he's in Rome, then the US, then in the Congo then—"

"OK, I get the point. Did you find anything useful?" I asked, frustrated. "No, not really," Dan replied.

I sighed into the receiver. "OK, keep me posted." "So does that mean I'm on the payroll now?" "No," I said then hung up the phone.

I walked into my gun room and flicked the lights on. It was underground, converted from a garage that was not needed. I began to load rounds for my pistol. At times it could be a mind-numbing job, but it allowed me time to think, time to drift off in a random direction that I would not have thought of otherwise.

I gently placed a polished 124-grain hollow-point projectile on top of a case and moved the lever through its arc, seating the slug on the powder. Carefully I lifted it out then sat back in my chair and studied it.

It looked brutal. I knew the ballistics and how the projectile mushroomed whenever it hit something substantial, like bone. I knew it created close on a four hundred foot pounds of energy and transferred nearly all that energy as it slammed into whatever it was aimed at. I also knew that being hit by one was not an experience I wanted to go through again. I touched the wound. It still hurt like hell occasionally, especially during the winter months. My shoulder had needed a near total reconstruction, and I'd endured months of rehabilitation.

I dropped the cartridge into a box alongside the forty-nine other rounds I had loaded. I pushed the lid on and wrote some numbers on the top denoting what they were and when they were loaded then locked them in a safe.

During the two hours I spent loading the cases, I couldn't think of anything new; JR44 was still a mystery, and Megan just added to the confusion. With the dust cover settled over the loading bench, I switched the light off and closed the door and locked it.

Tonight was not going to be my night.

Chapter 28

Kelly and Michelle walked across the garden area outside the common room. It was full of students eating lunch and talking about the latest gossip. They were best of friends and did everything together. They were almost joined at the hip—if someone saw one of them, then the other would not be far away. They waved to people as they strode purposefully towards the school gates. It was lunch hour, and being that they were seniors, they could leave the school grounds when they felt like it.

They walked across the grass of the school rugby field, headed towards the centre of town; it held a small café they liked to frequent. The owner was someone of questionable morals and he made no secret of the fact he liked to look at the young students. The two girls took advantage of this, hitching up their skirts just that little bit more and occasionally crossing their legs in his direction. This was often followed by knowing smiles, as they could see his reaction to their teasing, in his face and occasionally, elsewhere. The girls found this sort of flirting fun and it meant that he kept quiet about them smoking in his café. He wouldn't want to discourage his pretty little patrons, would he?

Their route led them along Centennial Drive. It wound its way through groves of trees and past man-made ponds covered in lilies. It was going to be a pleasant afternoon for both of them. Lunchtime meant the end of school for them; they had one more class after lunch, but neither of them had any intention of returning for it.

Michelle stopped and dug into her backpack for her packet of cigarettes. She offered one to Kelly as they stepped into a ring of trees that offered them protection from the public's prying eyes. Kelly dragged on her cigarette then looked at Michelle.

"Did you see that silly bitch in gym? Coordination is not her strong point."

Michelle nodded and bent over to look out and make sure they weren't going to be disturbed. As she bent over, Kelly glanced down. She couldn't help it. She could see the outline of Michelle's G-string pressed against the inside of her thin jeans. Kelly resisted the urge to reach out and stroke her beautiful curves. She turned away, her face flushing with colour.

Michelle straightened up again. "What should we do this afternoon?" Shrugging, Kelly looked out of a gap through the trees. People passed them by, only metres away, but they had no idea that they were there. She watched people walking in the distance and saw a face that she recognised.

But not one she wanted to come into contact with again.

"Do you remember Jakob?" Kelly asked, without turning around.

Michelle grabbed Kelly's shoulder and spun her around, in time to see the last of the red vanishing from her face. She ignored it. "We agreed that we wouldn't talk about him, remember?"

"Yes, I know that. But he's crossing the field over there and coming straight for us." Kelly pointed behind her at the field they had just crossed. Michelle peered through a gap in the leaves and saw him.

He was close. Jakob looked towards the trees the two girls he wanted to get his hands around had stepped into. They thought they were safe. He kept his head down and his eyes forward; he could taste their blood. Jakob could feel the small bat pressing into his back. He knew what he wanted to do, he wanted to make them suffer, make them fucking scream their pretty little heads off. It was nothing more than they deserved. Jakob was within twenty metres of them when he suddenly changed direction. He realised Kelly and Michelle were watching him; he could feel their gaze drilling into him. He wanted them to follow him.

Jakob looked back at the ring of trees and saw the slightest movement. He stopped and turned around. Jakob smiled to himself and told himself that he couldn't wait. His elaborate and sadistic plan for revenge was shoved to the back of his mind. He wanted blood, and he wanted it now.

Jakob ran, fast. He reached the trees and burst into the middle of the small clearing, startling Kelly and Michelle. Kelly dropped her cigarette onto the dry foliage, and Jakob looked down at it. A thought burst in his mind like a hand grenade.

"Kelly, Michelle. Just the people I was looking for," he started with a sly grin.

The two girls glanced at each other briefly and then back to Jakob. They had made a pact with each other and had agreed never to talk about the unpleasant moments spent by the river when they were much younger. They assumed that because Jakob had kept quiet that they would be in the clear, but now a sudden sickening feeling had descended over them like a cancer. Jakob scratched his head and looked at the girls.

"You do realise that it has been eleven years since you raped me with that stick by the river?" he asked almost casually. He delighted in watching their expressions change from surprise to fear. He wanted them to remember, wanted them to feel exactly what they were.

Jakob reached in to his pocket and pulled out a small piece of worn paper. He looked down at it and remembered vividly that day eleven years ago what he wrote on it. The girls stood watching him, carefully gauging his body language.

"I made a promise to myself that day. I promised myself that I wouldn't be humiliated or used like that ever again." He was still looking at the paper, but kept an eye on the girls in his peripheral, couldn't have them running off while he wasn't looking. The paper was so worn and dog-eared, the writing was almost illegible, but he knew what it said. He screwed his eyes shut and let the demons come to the surface. This was the day he had been waiting for, his day for vengeance.

"I made a promise to myself that I would destroy you both." His voice had taken on a growling quality.

He leapt forward and whipped the small bat from his pocket. His left foot hit the ground next to Michelle as he brought the bat around in an arc, crashing it into the side of her head just above her ear. There was a sickening crunch, and Michelle collapsed straight down onto the leaf-strewn dirt. Kelly stood wide-eyed and speechless, terror rooting her to the spot. Jakob turned and bore his gaze straight into her. The last thing she remembered was the sadistic evil sneer.

Jakob looked down at the two inert lumps of flesh lying at his feet, the sneer slowly fading from his face. He hefted the small bat in his hands then shoved it back into his pocket. He was going to make these two pay.

Jakob sat on the old sofa in the boarding room and watched the newscast in black and white. The school said they couldn't afford a coloured television for the students to watch, but they could afford to renovate the teachers' lounge. Jakob didn't care; he didn't watch it at all. He was more interested in staying away from the other freaks that inhabited the school after hours. But tonight he had to sit down and watch. He wanted to see if his handiwork had been found; he wanted to see what they would say.

"Tonight a grisly story about two girls found killed in a park near a secondary school. Then the weather for the weekend." Jakob sat quietly at the back of the room and waited for the newscast to start. He was filled with anticipation. In his ideal world, this would bring out the real truth of how cruel and mean the two girls had been to him, but he knew this would never come out. Still, in his mind, they had gotten back what they gave out . . . with interest.

"Tonight a grisly scene has been found in a park near Matamata College. Two girls were found brutally murdered and displayed in a macabre scene that could only have been thought up by a psychopath." Jakob smiled to himself as he remembered the hour it took him to tie the girls exactly how he wanted. He hadn't brought anything with him, so he had to improvise. "Police are not commenting on the crime, but it is believed that one of the girls is the daughter of a prominent horse breeder." The television flicked to a scene of a grove of trees surrounded with a red tape. Jakob watched the scene intently; he studied the trees to reassure himself that no one could have seen anything. He wanted them to show the two girls, wanted them to show the intimate position he had put them in. He knew about them. They thought they could keep it secret, but they underestimated him. He had watched them carefully; he knew their dirty little secret.

"It is believed that this may be the work of a local who has fallen out with the breeder in question. At this point in time, police are looking for evidence and early indications are that there are some prints in the soft dirt that may provide a lead."

Jakob's heart jumped. He swore quietly to himself as he desperately thought back to the scene. Another student turned to look at him so Jakob fixed a sinister gaze at him until he turned away. He returned his attention back to the television set and waited for more. As he waited his thoughts wandered back to yesterday afternoon. The memories both excited and relaxed him.

Jakob had pulled a small pen knife from his pocket and cut Kelly's top from her body. She lay unconscious in the dirt, a small trickle of blood flowing from her right ear. Jakob looked down on her, contempt filling his face which slowly turned to hate. He flicked his eyes to Michelle. She groaned and moved slowly in the dirt. Jakob stepped over Kelly's inert body and grabbed Michelle by her hair. He wrenched her head back and gazed into her unfocused eyes.

Michelle tried to focus on the face in front of her but couldn't. Her head throbbed like nothing she had ever felt. Jakob raised his fist and began to snarl. It ended in a deep low grating sound as he drove his clenched fist into her delicate cheek bone. The force of the blow fractured her eye socket and dislocated her jaw, but he knew none of this. He dropped Michelle onto the ground again and returned to Kelly.

Jakob finished tearing the clothes from them then set about carefully cutting the material into strips. He removed the wire from their bras and linked them together, making one long strand. He sat the girls back to back and wedged their socks into the mouths then tied their heads together with the wire. Jakob was just able to tie the loose ends of the wire together. He looked down at the pathetic couple and felt the briefest moment of compassion, but he quickly extinguished that thought when he reminded himself what they had done to him. Jakob brought Kelly's arms behind her and placed them in front of Michelle's stomach then laced them together with Michelle's G-string. He pulled it tight enough to cut the circulation to her wrists and then he did the same to Michelle. The picture in his mind was beginning to take shape. He tied their ankles together then sat back and waited for them to wake up.

Chapter 29

Megan powered up her laptop. She sat at her desk at the police station on Buscomb Avenue. It was early; her meeting with Spangle36 had been interesting, but she still wasn't sure she'd done the right thing. It could cost her job. It had kept her awake most of the night; she was beginning to feel the lack of deep sleep. Her computer chimed a good morning, and she deliberately ignored her e-mail. She opened an Internet browser and logged onto a chat room. She read some of the threads that were available, nothing jumped out at her. But that was the problem; she knew that if she didn't investigate every thread, then she would probably miss what she was looking for. She clicked on the first item and began the tedious study of the comments.

She spent four hours staring at the screen of her computer. She blinked and realised how sore her eyes were from the constant strain. Carefully, she leaned back in her chair and rubbed her tired eyes. A knock at her door startled her, Captain Holmes strode in uninvited.

"I hope you have something for me, Megan. I am starting to get calls from higher-placed individuals asking about our progress. Individuals I don't want to piss off."

Dropping a look that clearly said "I don't care," Megan stood up and walked out of the room, leaving the captain standing in her empty office. She poured herself a cup of coffee from the pot then walked back, taking her time. Walking back into her office, she found Holmes sitting in her chair. She slammed the door behind her. She was in the mood for an argument, and Captain Holmes had pushed her too far. Megan placed her coffee cup on the desk and gazed at him for a moment.

"Sir," she started off. She stopped to think of her next words. "I'm trying to find this person at the moment, but so far, we don't have a whole lot to work with." She stopped there and waited for the inevitable tirade of complaints to start.

"That's not good enough, Megan, you are paid more than most in this department, and we expect results."

He had said "we" as if someone was backing him up. Megan knew that the powers that be would be coming down on him like a tonne of bricks if he couldn't produce the results.

"You need to do something and soon. Remember your job is on the line for this, Megan." Holmes stood up as if to leave.

Megan slammed her fists on the desktop, knocking over her coffee. It flooded off the edge of the table and stained the new carpet.

"Don't you threaten me, asshole. I'll give you something when I find something, so back off and stay out of my way," she spat.

Holmes leant backwards in her leather seat. It was a side of her that he hadn't seen, and it caught him by surprise. She had been all over the place lately. These cases had gotten under her skin, done some damage, he could tell.

To Megan's surprise, the captain stood up and stalked out of the office. Megan sat back in her seat and ran her slender fingers through her hair in frustration. She knew she hadn't heard the last of that.

Megan clicked on her e-mail and saw a handful of messages, one from her parents in Russia, another from her brother. She also had one from a person whose address she didn't recognise. She clicked open the e-mail and began reading.

Dear Madam. It is believed that there are people within the greater Auckland area that mean to do me harm. I do not wish to be the one to point the finger at people, but when my own safety is threatened then I must take action. I believe you know the person I am talking about. He is a vigilante that seems to think he has the right to eliminate those that seek only justice for wrongdoings done. I hereby formally ask you to investigate and if possible to apprehend Emery Blackstone. I have complete faith that the New Zealand Police will do everything within its power to bring him to justice.

Megan leaned back in her seat and read the letter again. If she didn't know better, she would have actually bought it. She knew exactly who it was from. She hit the Return key and wrote a letter back.

Dear Sir. It is not Emery Blackstone you should worry about. If we cross paths again, I can guarantee that you will never have to worry about anything ever again.

She didn't bother signing it. It was bad enough she was sending it from a work address.

Chapter 30

Jakob sat in the trees looking at the two naked girls in front of him. He was disgusted by them. Their very existence repulsed him, but with them as they were, it made it almost unbearable for him. He gawked at their breasts and wondered what possible use these two could have for them. He vowed to himself that they would be among the first things he would remove. But before that he would cut out their tongues and put a small slit in their throats, rendering their voices useless. He wanted to inflict as much pain as he possibly could.

Jakob stood up and slapped Michelle across the face.

"Wake up," he whispered. Michelle's eyes fluttered then jammed open. She tried to scream, but the sock only choked her. Jakob's grinning face filled her vision.

"There is no point screaming. Soon you won't be able to make a sound," he said as he pulled a small blade from his pocket. He flicked the handle, and the blade snapped away from the body of the handle. He crouched down and pushed the blade up against Michelle's cheek. She began to whimper, stifled by the wire and sock gag.

"Do you like what you see, Michelle? Do you like what you see here or do you prefer little girls? Oh, wait a minute . . ." Jakob's face lit up with a big grin. "That's it. Now I know. You like Kelly. Or is it the other way round? She likes you, but you don't want that sort of relationship with her. You don't like a woman's taste, don't you?" Jakob hissed.

He pushed the blade into her cheek, slicing it open. She squealed, and her eyes rolled back in their sockets.

Jakob watched a trickle of blood run down her cheek, and his desire to kill her increased a hundredfold. He couldn't stop himself; the blade seemed to move by itself, across her throat. A splash of blood trickled then flowed freely, cascading down her front. Jakob stood mesmerised by the sight. He stood very still watching, waiting for it to stop gushing from the wound; eventually the flow reduced to nothing more than a seep. He stepped over her legs and turned to look Kelly straight in the eye.

"Michelle is dead. You're next," he stated in a dark voice. Jakob raised the blade and brought it level with her horrified gaze. He wasn't interested in taking revenge now; he wasn't interested in causing them pain. He only wanted to watch them die. Fast, slow, it didn't matter. The end result would be the same. Kelly eyed the blade, her eyes pleading, but no sound escaped her clogged throat.

Jakob cocked his head to one side, and the grin disappeared from his face. The movement was swift and savage; he shot his arm out straight and aimed the knife for Kelly's left temple. He hit her with such force that the blade drove in to the hilt of the handle. Kelly's legs began to spasm; she kicked a half-dozen times while Jakob held the blade. He pushed it in harder and twisted the handle, the bone resisting any movement. Kelly went rigid, and then her limbs stopped moving. Jakob checked her pulse then felt for a pulse on Michelle's neck.

Nothing, they were both gone. He sat back amongst the trees with a grin of satisfaction spreading over his face. He had finally exacted revenge on them, and to him, it felt better than he had ever imagined. Jakob stood up and gazed through a gap in the branches. He couldn't see anyone walking across the field. He stepped towards a gap then turned back to look at Kelly and Michelle.

"Good-bye, I hope you rot in hell," he said cheerfully and then disappeared.

Chapter 31

I sat in the dark, watching, waiting. Frustration and boredom were beginning to take hold, so I stood up and moved down the street a bit further, moving from shadow to shadow. The night was cold and dank; I could feel the restless city waiting for another day. I rounded a corner and looked hard into the gloom. My hand instinctively went to the holster at my back. I could feel the reassuring presence of my pistol and stepped forward into the darkness. Mathew and Jeff walked back from town. They were drunk, seriously drunk, and they both knew that a thumping hangover was waiting for them in the morning. Jeff looked at Mathew, who was concentrating on putting one foot in front of the other. He then turned back to look down the street in to the dark just as it started raining. The drops were cold, and very soon the pair were shivering but not really noticing it.

"Ha. Hey, Mathew," Jeff said in a drunken slur. Mathew stopped midstride and looked at Jeff, saw that he was pointing at something, then followed his arm in that general direction. There was a homeless man sitting on the sidewalk, leaning up against the brickwork of a bank building. It was two o'clock in the morning; no traffic was around except for the occasional reveller trying to get home before the sun came up again.

Jeff and Mathew stepped into the torrential flow in the gutter, their clothes already dripping wet, and crossed the street, towards the homeless man. Mathew stopped on the edge of the opposite sidewalk and swayed dangerously. Jeff stumbled up next to him, and they both looked down at the man leaning against the building, head down and trying to get what shelter he could from the rain.

"Hey you, drunken bum, get away from that building. You can't sleep there," Mathew called in as sober a voice as he could muster.

The guy had his head down and was under some sheets of crumpled news print. His eyes stayed closed. Jeff walked up and kicked the man in the leg. He moved on the concrete abruptly then settled back down again. Mathew looked at Jeff then they both looked down at the motionless body on the ground. Mathew drew his leg back for another kick when a sudden shock of electricity ripped through him. His body went rigged and convulsed a few times then fell to the wet pavement. The alcohol slowed his reactions to the point that he could do nothing to arrest his fall. He fell backwards, smashing his skull on the edge of the pavement and knocking him unconscious.

Jeff could do nothing but watch. His reactions were slowed even more, and it took him a long second to realise what was happening. He cranked his head to the side and saw his friend fall to the ground. Then he turned back to see the man dressed in old clothes standing before him. Jeff took a half a step back and looked straight into the eyes of the man in front of him and knew he was in serious trouble. Without warning, the man flicked his arm out, a flash of light bouncing off a steel blade. Jeff felt, more than saw, something hit him. He didn't register the pain at all. His hands automatically clutched at his stomach, and he looked down as he felt something warm and sticky.

The man smiled as another flash of light arced in front of Jeff's face. This time the pain hit him; he panicked and tried to scream but couldn't— only a choked gurgle escaped. His hand shot to his throat and was instantly covered in blood sheeting from the slit in the thin skin. Jeff fell to the pavement in a heap and the man watched him expire.

He turned his attention to Mathew, just a slight shift of his eyes. He was going to send her a message.

Chapter 32

I walked from shadow to shadow trying to avoid the street lights as much as possible. Then it started raining.

"Fuck..." I cursed quietly. Within seconds the road surface was soaked, torrents of water were heading for the grating set into the side of the road, and plunging down to the depths beneath the city streets. I stepped into the rain and crossed the empty street quickly. My gaze dropped to the footpath and I began to think I may never meet JR44. So far Megan hadn't been able to turn up anything other than an IP address. As I suspected it turned out to be a decoy. I paid a visit to the physical address it was registered to, but found only an empty storefront. We were going to need a break—and soon—otherwise this guy's trail was going to go cold. The break was about to come sooner than I thought.

I walked along the street, with my head down and eyes fixed six feet in front of me. I could sense it was getting close to dawn and decided to call it a night. It was going to take me an hour to drive home, and the night had been dead with nothing I would call serious coming my way.

I stopped on my way back towards my car, it was parked down a side alley adjacent a hostel. Up ahead of me was a service station bathed in bright fluorescent light. I could see one car parked next to the pumps, and presumably it was the owner that was now frantically thumping on the attendant's window. She seemed far too lively for this hour of the morning. I could hear her screaming at him, though I couldn't make out the words. I crossed the street again, this time not noticing the rain. As I got closer to the woman, I could hear her yelling something about a man that had hung himself, but the horrified look on her face told me there was more to what she was saying. I walked up to her and asked, "Ma'am, what's wrong?"

She turned to me, her eyes wide with fear. She said nothing, just pointed down the street; I followed her arm and balked at the sight. From across the street where I had been I wasn't able to see around the shallow bend in the road towards the traffic lights. But now I could see what the lady had been so frantic about.

A man was hanging from one of the tall, arching lamp posts that lined the road. The light was shaped like a giant letter L that had been pushed into the ground upside down, so the he was hanging out over the street. From this distance, it looked like he was hung with rope but it was hard to tell, the weak dawn light was still not strong enough to define anything.

I started across the street again towards the man. Another car had stopped and a man stepped out of the driver's seat, looking up as he did. He promptly bent over and vomited on the ground. I picked up the pace and jogged to the front of the man's car.

"Are you all right?" I asked.

The man didn't reply, just nodded, still head down and doubled over. It was then that I looked up and saw for the first time the gravity of the situation. The man had been hung all right, but with looked like his own intestines. I felt my stomach lurch sideways but managed to regain control.

I looked away from the grisly sight and around the immediate area. Rubbish lay up against the building nearby and paper lay scattered, soaked in the rain. I moved away and into the shelter from the eve of the building. It was then that I saw a foot sticking out from underneath the pile of paper. I pulled the pistol from its holster and yanked the slide back. As the bolt slammed home the pile of papers moved.

I stepped forward and kicked the pile hard.

"Get up!" I yelled. The pile moved and then an arm snaked its way out, pushing the papers back, and revealing a garden-variety homeless man. He rubbed sleep out of his eyes and looked up at me. He was covered in grime, and I could smell him even though I had stopped six feet away.

"Wha' you want, man?" he asked in a slur. I relaxed my grip on the pistol but keep it drawn. I pointed at the gruesome sight behind me. The homeless man traced my arm and his eyes fell open.

"I had nothing to do with tha'," he insisted, shaking his head. "Never said you did, you see or hear anything?"

The man shook his head again. "Nah man, been sleep right here all nigh'." He paused for a second as he thought about something. I kept quiet and waited for him to continue.

"I come back from town, and some asshole stole my spot. You see its unwritten law, the code y'know? You don't go stealing other street folks' spots. I turned up and someone had taken it, so I had to sleep round the corner. In the rain. I didn' hear anything but decided to come back and tell the thief where to go, but he wasn' here. Certainly didn' see that either." He was pointing at the corpse hanging from the street lamp. I bent down and gazed into the man's eyes.

"Hey, man, I swear I had nothing to do with it," he pleaded.

I stood up but kept my gaze on him. Removing my phone from my coat pocket, I dialled Megan; she answered after the third ring.

"What?" she asked without greeting.

"We have a problem. There has been another one. Great North Road, Eden park end, opposite the service station. I think you need to see this," I said quietly into the phone.

"I'm on my way," she replied quickly and then the line went dead.

I clicked my phone shut and dropped it back into my pocket. Surveying the scene once again, something felt wrong. I walked down the street a bit further and looked down a long alleyway, the gloom still quite deep. I looked up at the rapidly-lightening sky; it was going to be another bleak day in the city of sails. I looked back towards the man lying on the sidewalk. He remained where he was, still under the pile of rubbish. I guess even a corpse hanging from the street lights wasn't going to make him give up his spot.

I walked between the buildings into the gloom. I could barely make out the scattered rubbish bins overflowing with waste, which were lined up along the edges of the shops. Thirty paces into the darkness I discerned a lump on the ground. It wasn't consistent with the rest of the contents of the alley which made it stand out. I moved slowly towards it, carefully placing each foot so as not to disturb anything.

It was then the sickly sweet coppery smell of blood hit me. It wasn't overpowering, but it was enough to tell me that there was something very wrong here.

I backed away from the second body and walked back into the lightning grey of the morning. I blinked a few times as my eyes adjusted, and looked around the surrounding area, I couldn't see any cameras mounted in discreet places; obviously this wasn't a high risk area. I looked across the road at the service station. Even though the storefront was in the line of sight, it was only out by a fraction. I walked back across the road in the easing rain towards the service station front window.

By now, the attendant had his doors open and was standing on the forecourt watching the scene unfold. I walked slowly towards him and stopped a few feet away.

"Don't suppose you saw anything, did you?"

The young guy turned his head towards me, long hair partially covering his eyes. I looked at him. His clothes hung off his gaunt shoulders, and his eyes clouded by the abuse of something illegal. I didn't like my chances of finding out anything useful from him. The guy held my gaze for a few seconds then looked away, back at the scene. I could hear sirens wailing in the distance.

"You know, the cops are going to ask you the same questions. And they might take one look at you and ask a few more questions. They might even ask you if you are on something."

That got his attention. The guy looked at me, not with nervous eyes, but a hard and steely glare. "Are you accusing me of something?" he asked in well spoken English.

I shook my head. "Nope, but understandably, first appearances can deceive." I nodded outside. "I noticed on the way in that there is a camera pointed in that direction. I know the distance is quite large, but can I see the footage?"

The service station attendant looked at me sideways. "Are you a cop?" "No."

"Isn't that like contaminating the evidence of a scene or tampering with evidence in a police investigation?" he asked.

I could see where this was going; he was going to make it difficult.

"I may not be a cop, but you are impeding the investigation of a serial killer. One who obviously came close to here, and one who is indiscriminate in who he kills. If you show me the tape I'll tell the cops that you saw exactly zero and I'll be on my way. If, however, you decide to fuck me around, I will quietly suggest to my friends in the police that they might want to search the premises. I don't think the owners will be very happy about that, particularly if they find something."

I could see the guy thinking, finally deciding that it would be in his best interests to cooperate. He turned on his heel and walked back into the shop. I followed him, through an aisle, and out to the rear, through a door marked Staff Only. He turned to a door on his left and pulled a set of keys from his pocket, dug through them, found the right one then pushed it into the lock.

"Its old equipment but it does the job. The insurance company say they want us to upgrade but haven't given us a solid reason why yet." I nodded and looked at the old tape recorder. I hadn't seen one of these in years. Mostly people upgrade to digital image software, basically recording it straight to a hard drive on a computer. It makes life a lot simpler if you have to scroll through it to find something, like I was about to.

"Are you sure you didn't see anything at all. No strange people acting suspiciously earlier this morning?" I asked. The guy rolled his eyes at me and shook his head.

"OK. Show me how to use this, would you," I said pointing at the archaic recorder.

"Are you sure, you know it looks about as old as you are." the guy said with a faint hint of a grin. I shot the little punk an icy stare and he shut up then busied himself with setting it up.

"This thing records on a loop, so not all the footage will be on here." "How long is that then? Will it have, say, back to midnight?" I asked. "Yeah, the loop is eight hours long. We swap it out every shift and store the tapes. That is one reason the insurance company is trying to get us to switch to computers. The volume of tapes created, plus they become unreliable once they are used a few times."

I looked at the screen, it was a blank blue. Every now and then a white line would whip through it as fast as I could blink. The attendant popped a tape into another player and pressed play. He switched a button on the television and a grainy picture flooded the screen. A shot of the fore court bathed in fluorescent light flicked past, then onto a shot of inside the shop.

I could see the guy sitting in the corner reading a magazine, and then it flicked away again to another shot of the street. I could only just see the street corner in the upper left hand corner of the screen. It was difficult to make out.

"Can you zoom in on this area here?" I asked, pointing at the area in question.

The guy looked at me. "This isn't a computer, what you see is what you get." He replied.

I looked down at him as the screen jumped away again.

"OK then, I'm going to need that tape so I can sit down with a bowl of popcorn and enjoy the quality movie," I said sarcastically. "You're reluctance to help is becoming quite annoying, so just go along and we'll fucking get along, OK."

The guy shrugged his shoulders and hit eject. The recorder spat the tape out and he jammed it in a dust cover then handed it to me.

"Does this cover from midnight to now?" I asked. The guy nodded and said nothing.

"OK, you'll get this back when I'm finished with it." I turned and headed for the door.

I walked outside into the morning air. A few more people were out and about. A police car had parked sideways and was blocking the street. I looked to my right and saw two police cars parked nose to nose across the street blocking traffic in both directions from the Northern motorway and Great North Road. The street was largely deserted, except for around the area of the corpse. Police stood around looking up at the man, I figured they were waiting for a cherry picker or scissor lift to arrive so they could get a better look. Procedure meant they'd probably have to leave it dangling in public view until the forensics team showed up too.

I stepped off the sidewalk onto the street, the rain had subsided to a light drizzle and a shaft of light was making an attempt to break through the low cloud.

A plainclothes car and a marked van pulled up. Megan jumped out of the car and headed for whoever was in charge. A quick conversation ensued, ending as she pointed around at the various alleys off the street, including the one I had found the second body in. I carefully placed the tape in my jacket and zipped it up. As far as I was concerned, the police didn't need to know about the tape just yet.

"Sir, you can't go there. It's a crime scene and we need you to get back out of the cordon." I turned to look at the person approaching me. He would have been all of twenty years old, five foot six, and probably weighed 150 pounds sopping wet with his shoes still on. I ignored him and kept walking towards Megan.

"Sir, I'll ask you again to get back; otherwise I'm going to have to arrest you for obstruction."

I stopped in my tracks and turned to look at the little punk. My attitude was beginning to turn bad. I looked hard at him as he was walking towards me; he slowed his pace stopping out of reach. I stood my ground and said nothing.

"Sir, I won't ask you again," he stated in a louder voice. I figured he was hoping that the others would hear and come running to back him up. "I'm going to walk over there and see Ms. Webb. She is one of the detectives in forensics. If you have any objections, I suggest you talk to her. I believe she is running the scene, in case you didn't know." I turned and carried on walking. He started to say something again, but I ignored him again. I wasn't in the mood to be pleasant. I caught Megan's eye, and she began to walk over.

"It's OK, Sergeant, he's a part of this investigation," she called out as she pulled me to one side. She turned her back on him and literally pushed me across the street to her car and out of the rain.

"Get in," she told me flatly.

I walked around the passenger side and climbed in. It was warm and dry inside her car but wouldn't be much longer with me dripping all over her seat.

"You shouldn't be here, Emery. You've caused enough shit as it is." She checked her rear-view mirror to see who was watching. I turned and looked out of the rear window. No one was paying her the least bit of attention. Not with that poor chap to stare at.

"Well, it's not like I planned to be here," I replied.

"That guy," she said, pointing out the window, "has been hung with his intestines." She screwed her face up.

"They aren't his."

Megan turned to look at me, startled out of her disgust. There was a knock at the window, and she turned to see a sergeant dressed in a raincoat, and looking in at her expectantly. She slid the window down a fraction and waited for him to talk.

"Ma'am, we have found another body, in one of the alleyways. He's been gutted. There's nothing left. It's awful—looks like the killer used his mate's insides to string the other one up."

That screwed-up expression settled back on her face. The officer left her staring at the horn symbol on the steering wheel of her car.

"You have to stop him. He's getting out of control," I stated. No response. "Do you have a video player?"

She turned and looked at me. "What?"

"A VHS player, I had a little chat to the guy across the road at the service station. I got this." I pulled the cassette from my jacket. "It might have some footage of the crime scene. Something we can use to pin him down with, because at the moment he hasn't left us a lot except a big middle finger."

Megan looked at the tape as if it were from outer space.

"You think the killer might be on there?" she asked doubtfully.

"It's worth a shot, because at the moment we don't exactly have much to go on. Why, for example, has he now chosen a couple of men? I thought pretty girls were his thing?"

"He's showing off. No other reason for such a public display. He knows I'd be one of the first here."

She turned to look outside, paused, and then threw her door open. I watched her climb out and run the few short paces to one of the senior officers. She said something I couldn't quite make out, and the cop nodded. When she returned to the car, she looked more composed. The slammed the door shut.

"Let's go and see if we can find him."

Chapter 33

Megan pulled up and into the driveway of her house. It was getting on to nine o'clock in the morning and I was feeling tired. I hadn't slept for close to twenty four hours. I'd barely eaten, and I could feel bile biting the back of my throat as my stomach protested in frustration. I opened the passenger door and climbed out.

The clouds were breaking overhead but still coming thick and fast. The wind had begun to pick up and I got the feeling that today was going to be a long day. I looked across the roof of the car at Megan. Her freshly washed hair was carefully styled over her shoulders, and she looked composed, but I could see the stress and a few late nights were beginning to get to her.

"Maybe we should get something to eat first," I suggested.

Megan looked back at me as she walked up the short path to the front door. "I'm OK, I've already eaten."

"That's good because I haven't," I replied caustically. She stopped and looked at me, confusion lining her face.

"Sorry, I'm tired and hungry. This would possibly be the only time I wouldn't refuse a coffee either." I guess my tired attempt at a smile said it all. She beckoned me towards her house; I followed her up the stairs and inside. Inside it smelt like the remnants of hot showers and warm toast. The smell of shampoo hung faintly in the air. I followed her through the hallway and into the kitchen. It was small but well organised. I saw a trace of print powder on a surface that must have been forgotten to be cleaned.

"There's bread in the fridge, the toaster is under the counter and there," she said pointing at a dark coloured ceramic container, "is the coffee." She disappeared into the lounge and left me standing in front of the sink.

"Thanks." I mumbled quietly to myself. Pulling the toaster out and placing it on the bench, I kept thinking about this morning. While the kettle was boiling, I retrieved the bread and peeled off a couple of slices. Why would someone go through the trouble of hanging a man like that? He would have been totally exposed for a lengthy period of time, and the only real chance was the homeless man who seemed reluctant to do anything. I only hoped the security footage would reveal something useful.

The kettle clicked off and the toast popped as I heard the television come on. The lounge was sparsely furnished; only what she required. I guessed she spent most of her time behind a desk or out at a crime scene which it seemed, well to me anyway. I sat down in an empty single seater and watched her fumble around behind her television disconnecting and reconnecting cables. She had an old video player sitting on the floor in front of the box and was trying to get it to run.

"Damn it. Is there any picture?" she asked.

"No, not yet," I said around a mouthful of toast. She pulled a cable out and the television started making a horrible humming noise that

I thought didn't sound very good, then it vanished and a blank screen appeared.

"That's it." The room became quiet. She pushed the tape into the machine and hit play on the recorder. It made a whirring sound then an image of the forecourt at the service station appeared. It was bathed in bright fluorescent light; no one was in the shot. I could see rain at the edges of the roof that covered the pumps and in the street. It flicked past and was replaced with a shot of the store. The attendant sat behind the counter reading a magazine, I couldn't tell what kind but the large, rounded shapes on the pages, and the way he was reading it, suggested porn. It flicked away and was replaced with a shot of the street. Again, in that very top left corner, I could see the street light. I looked at the time stamp at the bottom of the screen, it said it was twenty minutes past midnight.

"The murders would have happened at least an hour and a half, maybe two hours before I arrived. That would make it around four in the morning," I said, picking up my second piece of toast.

Megan nodded and touched the fast forward button. The time stamp moved quickly but not quick enough. The screens flicked past in a crazy dance of the shots the security cameras captured. She took her finger off the button after a minute or so, and an hour had elapsed. We watched it for a few minutes as a car pulled up to the pumps. The driver got out and walked up to the security window. I couldn't tell what was going on but I guessed the person was buying some fuel. We watched the person fill the car then get in and drive off.

Then nothing.

Nothing for another hour. Megan stabbed the button again and the wobbly dance of pictures started again. I sat there slowly sipping my coffee. It tasted raw and vile but I could feel the caffeine working on my sleep-deprived brain. She pressed the button again and the normal picture resumed, flipping through three sets of images in which nothing happened.

"Must have been a slow night." I noted.

Megan didn't answer; remaining focused on the screen. She grew tired of watching nothing and pressed the button again. I watched as time accelerated past. It grew close to three o'clock in the morning when she hit the play button again. This time we sat for more than half an hour watching as random people walked up to the window and bought something. From their dress, most looked as though they were on their way home from a night on the town.

It wasn't until the time hit three forty-three that something interesting happened. During a shot of the street lamp, I could see the homeless guy walk past like he said. He was wearing the same shabby coat and hat, which was pulled down low over his eyes. He had his head down and was walking slowly, but I thought he looked like he was walking with some intention. Not what I would have guessed a person of the street would be walking like, too much confidence. Even though his head was down, his shoulders were back and he walked with large, slow strides. He wasn't the bumbling drunk I'd spoken with earlier.

"Who are you?" I asked, not expecting an answer. Megan turned and looked at me, then back at the screen.

"Could be our guy." She supposed. "Maybe."

We continued watching in silence. The image skipped in between shots and I paid attention to only the top left corner. I could see some activity near the street lamp but nothing that really caught my eye. I watched the homeless man walk into shot and disappear down the alleyway where I had discovered the second body. He returned three screens later to take his spot under the pile of newspapers and rubbish near the building adjacent to where the body was found. I sat forward and watched the screen intently. It took another thirty minutes for something to happen. Two pedestrians walked into shot, obviously intoxicated. They crossed the street then disappeared from shot as it flipped to another screen.

"Fuck, that's them! Speed it up," I said as I leaned forward.

Megan skipped forward at a slower pace and played it at a shot of the street. The two guys were standing over the homeless guy. It clearly showed one of them kicking the shapeless form under the pile of rubbish, then the picture changed back to the bright forecourt again. I waited while nothing happened, before giving way to yet another shot of the punk behind the counter. Before it went back to the street, my patience was already beginning to erode.

When the shot jumped back to the road, I focused hard on the top left hand corner and watched the activity unfold. The shapeless form under the pile of rubbish had risen to his feet, and within a few seconds of the shot coming on the screen, he exploded and lunged at one of the pedestrians. The pedestrian went down hard, landing half on the road and half on the pavement. The second guy only staggered and watched, his swaying shadow evident even on the bad video. I watched the homeless man carefully. Something was vaguely familiar. Movement caught my attention. His arm swung through an arc twice, and the guy's dark form sunk to the ground. The screen flipped away again.

"Damn it." Megan pressed the fast forward button and brought the next screen shot of the street up. The guy stood over the two inert bodies looking down at them, and then he looked up at the lamp pole.

"I guess that's him then. But that bum seemed adamant that he had nothing to do with it." I said quietly. The picture skipped forward then stopped. Megan looked closely at the screen.

"I've seen him somewhere before," she said. I looked at the screen then back at her.

"Can you remember where?" I asked. If this guy on screen felt vaguely familiar to both Megan and I, then he was playing a dangerous game. Stringing both of us into his perverted game was not a good idea.

She closed her eyes and began whispering to herself. I sat quietly and waited, hoping that she would be able to give us a break. She began shaking her head slowly.

"No, it's right there in front of me but I can't see it," she said as she opened her eyes again.

"I think we need to go back and look more closely at the crime scene again." I said as I finished my coffee. Megan turned and looked at me.

"You can't. You're every cop's dream catch. You don't need to draw any more attention to yourself than you did this morning." She stood up.

"Then drop me off close by, and I'll scout around, see if I can find anything out of the ordinary."

"Emery, that's suicide, or stupidity. The area will be locked down and officers will be crawling everywhere. I'm surprised you didn't get arrested earlier."

"Don't argue with me Megan. Either I come with you right into the middle of it all, or you drop me off and I'll look around, your choice."

She rolled her eyes and shook her head but didn't protest, just ejected the tape and began walking for the door.

Chapter 34

Jakob strode down the sidewalk. He was sure now that he had her full and complete attention. The message he had scribed in the man's chest was sure to take care of that. He was in the centre of town; he had no need to hang around and watch the police contaminate the crime scene. He had seen them perform that adequately before.

The bum had played his part superbly, almost to perfection. The two hundred dollars and bottle of whiskey had been enough of an incentive for him to do the job exactly as he had told him to. The dolt could barely keep his filthy hands off him when he told him the deal. Jakob wasn't sure he'd understood even half of what was said; still it did and would have the desired effect.

One nagging bother to Jakob's current happy state was Emery. He was beginning to become more of a threat than a mere nuisance. Still, he was certain that they didn't have a clue who he was, or what he looked like, except maybe for the brief conversation with Megan in Hamilton. Jakob quickly pushed the small seed of doubt from his mind.

"No, definitely not." He shook his head as he whispered to himself. He had been more than careful up to this juncture. If there was anything the years had taught him, it was to cover his tracks. He had seen others like him come and go, every so often appearing on the news accompanied by pictures of beautiful, young girls. They'd usually get caught after doing something stupid. Some were even stupider. Their lust would overcome them, and suddenly the seventeen-year-old girl that had been looking at them across the bar was really a very young twenty-year-old woman, with a badge and a gun.

He recalled one young comrade. Though, he was of particular interest to Jakob and he had learnt a lot from his flamboyant style. The young man, who only went by the name Nick, was being hunted high and low by the police. But they never managed to catch him.

Nick came to town with a big entrance. Here was a truly psychopathic terrorist, and beautifully clever about it. Some of the murder scenes were pure art.

A member of the public, pursuing something of illicit means, spotted a man leant at an unusual angle under the main harbour bridge. Investigating, he walked in a little closer and noticed something unusual hanging from the man's lips. The passer-by checked his watch. He was going to be late for his pick up, but curiosity got the better of him. He moved closer, losing sight of him momentarily as he climbed over some rocks. The passer-by climbed over the last rock then stopped dead in his tracks, his eyes wide, a choked breath caught in his throat.

The man was dead. He was strung between two posts, sitting down with his legs crossed and his arms out. His throat had been cut and the tongue had been pulled through the slit like a morbid neck tie. But what made the passer-by vomit were his genitals hanging from his mouth. Post mortem results would show that the man's lips had been sewn shut around the penis.

Jakob remembered reading the article in the Herald. The police had said they had a number of leads to follow, although no one had been charged yet. Jakob remembered thinking that the end would come soon for Nick.

And as quickly as Nick had arrived, he disappeared. His abandoned apartment was eventually discovered, and enough evidence found to shock families about the habits of their "nice, quiet" boy. His body was never found, though. Jakob thought to himself that if he got the opportunity, he would ask Emery if he knew anything about it.

Jakob stopped at a street corner, looked left, then right. People stopped beside him and he began to fantasize about Megan. He was getting impatient with waiting, he wanted her now, for his own, to do with what he pleased. The crosswalk light turned green and someone walked into him from behind, the impact pushed Jakob off the sidewalk and into the gutter.

He turned and looked at the offender.

"Why don't you watch where you're going idiot?" The offender said to him. Jakob instantly dropped his head and stepped to one side. The man walked past without a second glance. Jakob turned and watched him go.

"You're lucky I don't slit your throat, right here right now asshole." Jakob mumbled. His temper flared up dramatically but he managed to keep it from exploding. Thoughts of the man's blood spraying across the road and draining towards the gutter suppressed his rage briefly. Just as the light turned red Jakob stepped onto the street and began to run across the road, out of the way of traffic.

He decided as he reached the other side that he would not let it go.

CHAPTER 35

Megan pulled her car up to the cordon blocking the road and rolled down her window a fraction. It was cold and blustery, but at least the rain had stopped. She flashed the officer her identification and the cop motioned towards me. Megan turned to him and talked her way through, calling me a consultant. A smile crept across my face. Consultant, I'd never been called that before. She let her foot off the brake, and we coasted forward to stop behind a squad car. She turned to me with her game face on.

"Don't talk to anyone. If someone asks you a question, tell them to see me. I'm leading this team here and everything has to come to me first."

I nodded and didn't say anything. She opened the door and stepped into the cold morning air. I followed suit and took in the surrounding area again, this time in a better light. I sighed; today was going to be a long day. Megan walked off towards the forensics unit; I stood by the car and watched. Looking back at the forecourt of the service station, I noted that it was a little busier at this time of day. Three cars sat parked on the forecourt and two in parking slots next to the shop.

It occurred to me briefly that perhaps JR44 was sitting in the shop, maybe cheering us on as we tried to find him, all while he was only fifty metres away.

I shook my head and grinned; he was starting to consume too much of my time and my thoughts. I had pictured him numerous times looking at me, his eyes wide, mouth open choking for air as I strangled the life out of him. I hoped one day soon I would get to make that dream a reality.

Megan called out to me, breaking my reverie, as a truck pulled up to the police vehicle blocking the road. I ambled over to her keeping my head down, trying not to meet anyone's gaze or attract undue attention.

"We should be able to get the body down now," she said, pointing at the truck. I turned to look at it and then returned my attention to the alley. "Is there any sign of the homeless guy that was here?" I asked, scanning the sidewalk.

"One of the officers said he slipped away." She pointed towards the city.

I followed her arm towards the Sky tower. "Has anyone gone after him?" I asked.

"Not yet, I was going to send one of the younger officers after him." "Don't bother, I'll go." I said. "I got a good look at him."

Megan nodded and started towards the truck with the scissor-lift tied to the back of its deck. An officer drove it slowly and cautiously towards the area. They had been waiting almost an hour for the truck to arrive, as the rest of the world woke up and headed for work, their roadblocks were now causing major traffic jams along the motorway and Great North Road. As far as Megan was concerned however, this was a homicide investigation and they would have to wait. She was all business. I watched her walk away and decided the homeless guy could wait. I wanted to have a closer look at the man hanging from the light pole.

We watched the scissor-lift slowly rise up towards the dead man. There were three people on it, two officers and presumably the forensics guy. He'd have a lot of pressure on him to conduct a very quick investigation. Nobody wanted this guy still swinging when the news crews got wind of it.

The scissor-lift platform stopped with the dead man in the middle, I guessed that they hadn't let the body touch the floor yet. The officers stood back while the forensics guy moved in. He started by photographing the body as it was found. He got up close to the head and neck. He did a meticulous job, clearly frustrating the more senior officers waiting on the ground. I checked my watch. After twenty minutes, they decided to cut the man down.

The officers grabbed both sides of the man, under the arm and either side of his jeans. They gently took the weight while the forensics guy cut through the intestines supporting him. He must have been heavier than he looked as the officers nearly dropped him. I watched them lower him down onto the covered floor, and bring the lift down to the ground again. The timing was perfect, cameras arrived two minutes too late to show the breakfast viewers the source of the motorway snarl-up. Covers quickly went up around the area.

I heard a tearing sound like fabric. The forensics guy stood up and the two cops visibly recoiled, jumping back as if the body was still alive, or trying to kill them from beyond the grave. They slowly leaned back in closer to get a good look. The forensics guy began taking his photos again. He was pressing the button furiously. I looked at Megan; she had a confused expression lining her face.

"Marty, what is it?" she asked.

Everyone stopped what they were doing and turned to look up, waiting for an answer. Marty pulled out a cloth from his pocket and wiped his forehead even though the temperature was well below fifteen degrees. He looked at the body for a moment longer then looked down directly at Megan.

"The killer scribed a message in his chest. By the looks of the wounds, it was while he was still alive, before he was hung." He paused to look at the two officers, before continuing.

"Ah, Megan, the message, it's for you."

CHAPTER 36

Night fell over the city. Jakob looked out of the sixth floor apartment building in downtown Auckland. He loved the city; all its diverse inhabitants made it a colourful place to work. If he wanted, he could lose himself easily amongst the people. He lifted the binoculars to his eyes and gazed at the window across the street. The asshole that had walked into him at the crossing sat across the street, four stories up, in a conservatory sipping on a champagne glass. He was alone at the moment, but the three days he had been watching him told Jakob that he had at least two girls on the go. Jakob almost admired him for it, almost, if it weren't for the fact that he wanted him dead.

It was a Wednesday afternoon; Jakob had tailed the man to work, to a mall, to a strip club and to a restaurant. Jakob followed him into the restaurant choosing a table for two, near the back of the dining area, where he could watch both the man and the door at the same time. Jakob had been sitting for half an hour just watching, waiting. He'd ordered two coffees, and he got the impression that the wait staff were beginning to become impatient with him. Jakob ignored them and focused on his target.

Five minutes later, a blonde woman wearing an overly tight red dress, walked through the door. Pausing near the reception podium she looked straight past the wait staff, instead scanning the restaurant's seated guests. On spotting the man she was looking for, she waved out enthusiastically, and yelled his name out across the room. With a dress like that, there was no room for even an ounce of class.

A few of the men seated around the room turned to the source of the voice. Some were more subtle than others—depending on who they were dining with. Jakob couldn't help but notice that a few of them lingered more than was socially acceptable.

He watched the blonde traverse the room with a big smile on her face, never taking her eyes off the man she had come to see. She navigated the tables with practiced ease, and was soon embracing the man in a rather public display of affection. Jakob studied her body, she was tall and slim. He thought to himself that she obviously worked out. He couldn't help but notice her breasts; they almost overflowed the top of her dress.

Jakob sipped his coffee; it was already lukewarm going on cold. He decided not to order another one; instead he ordered the smallest dish they had. The mussels turned up forty minutes later. Jakob looked down at them and considered not eating them, just to spite the chef.

The man and the blonde ate a light dinner and talked for another half an hour over wine. Jakob sat and waited, he didn't have anywhere to be. He was about to order another coffee when they both stood and made their way to the door. Jakob slurped the coffee as he stood up. He left the mussels exactly where the waiter had placed them on the table. He was walking towards the door just as a crowd walked in. He figured if he timed it right he would be able to slip out onto the street and disappear without paying. And he did just that.

Jakob tailed the man and his lady friend back to the man's apartment. He watched them climb the stairs and the light bloom to life in his apartment.

Jakob turned and entered the building across the street and walked up to his room. He'd rented for the week, specifically asking for one with a view of the street.

Jakob sat next to the window and watched them until late in the evening. The man didn't bother pulling the curtain or lowering the blind when he led her into his bedroom. Jakob watched them undress each other and soon Jakob could feel emotions beginning to bubble.

The man laid the woman on the bed and slowly began kissing his way up her body. He stopped and paid particular attention to her, nuzzling below her stomach. Jakob zoomed in trying to get a better look. The woman arched her back off the bed, her legs bent and open. Jakob dropped the binoculars away; he hadn't noticed his breathing becoming deep and rapid, the hard lump in his trousers.

Jakob couldn't control himself. He had watched them for twenty minutes and wished he could be that man, wished he could be the one with his hands running over the taught body of the blonde. He concentrated hard on the scene unfolding in front of him and barely noticed his own hand snaking its way down. He didn't want to but he knew he couldn't help it.

Chapter 37

It was a few days later when both Megan and I walked into the morgue. I followed her lead through the doors into the stark white room. It was bathed in overly powerful fluorescent light that was particularly hard on the eyes after the darkened corridor. The first thing I noticed was the smell, decaying flesh fighting the disguise of strong bleach and disinfectant. The medical examiner walked to a wall covered with stainless steel doors. He read his way across them until he found the two bodies from Great North Road. He unlocked one of the doors and swung it open then reached in and grabbed a stainless steel handle. The tray rolled out and hit the stops with a clang.

"This is Jeff Allen. He was a science student at the university studying chemical engineering. From what I hear he was quite an intelligent student. He was near the top of the class."

I had already read the report, and knew everything the police had found out thus far, so that bit of information didn't interest me. The examiner pulled the stark white sheet back and revealed him. It struck me how seeing a corpse laid out like this was very different to seeing it fresh, cleaner, and somehow more real.

A twelve inch gash dominated his body; there was another smaller cut across his throat. The examiner pointed at this and said, "This was the cause of death. We found a large amount of alcohol in his blood, which, combined with the adrenaline surge that might have kicked in, would have caused his heart to pump faster than normal, and cause exsanguination quite rapidly. The cut across his abdomen was caused either at the same time, or only a few moments after the cut across his throat."

Megan looked down at the body. "Is that all that happened to him?"

The examiner nodded. He covered the body back up again, pushed the tray back into the chiller, and closed the door. He stepped to the next drawer to his left and opened it. Even refrigerated, the rotting stench was almost winning the battle over the disinfectant.

"This young man is Mathew North. Of the two, I think he was attacked first. The examiner opened the door and rolled the steel table out. He removed the cloth and looked down at the mutilated body.

"There are multiple sets of paired, pin point intrusions in two locations. One set of marks in his thigh, and another in his abdomen. Around each mark, it appears that the skin has suffered the light burn characteristics of Taser marks. I would say he was incapacitated very quickly with the first shots, I don't understand why there are more." He looked up at Megan and me as if to emphasise the point.

"He has then fallen backwards and hit the curb of the road with quite a lot of force. This resulted in cracking of the skull. A chip of bone the size of a ten cent piece was pushed backwards into his brain. This was the cause of death." He lifted the head of the bench, tilting it as he did so to show us more clearly.

Megan walked around and looked closely at the hole. There was a small trickle of blood but other than that it looked completely normal.

"The mark around his neck is indicative of being suspended for a significant period of time. First assessment on the scene was correct. He has been hung with Jeff's small intestine," he stated.

Megan nodded then looked down at the message carved into his chest. "What do you make of this?" she asked, indicating with her hand.

The ME looked down and stayed quiet for a moment. When he spoke, I thought I felt the temperature in the room drop a couple of degrees.

"The man who did this, quite simply, wants you dead. I haven't seen this kind of display here before. Not too many psychos on this level out there. But I do have colleagues abroad that I am regularly in contact with. I sent a quick call out, and have one response who says he has seen this kind of symbolism." he said as he looked at her.

Megan's lips tightened shut while her gaze became fixed on the bloody message.

"What do you mean by symbolism?" I heard her ask quietly.

"He thinks he can get to you wherever and whenever he wants. He's trying to prove that by using a random victim, and knowing that you are an investigator, he knew you would see it."

Megan turned and looked at me then back at the ME, a pained expression on her face. I took out a pen and pad and wrote down the message. I was sure she had already written it down somewhere, and there were probably hundreds of photos of it, but I wanted to take it for myself. We were getting nowhere fast with the investigation, and the bodies were piling up. I couldn't stick around too much longer with Megan; her colleagues were already asking more questions.

I had a bad feeling that things were about to get worse but I kept it to myself.

"This person knows how to kill people and kill efficiently. He knows where and when to strike and it appears that he can do it with minimal disturbance." The ME added.

Megan looked up. "What makes you think it's a he?"

"Typically, female serial killers are likely to use a covert means, poison, that kind of method. They tend to kill more for material gain than at random. This here looks like the person is trying to send you a message, of which I think he has succeeded. Plus, this looks like it is done out of rage, the brutal, repeated nature of the wounds, and being hung with his companion's intestines. I think it all points to a male," The ME replied matter-of-factly.

I touched Megan's shoulder and motioned to her that we should go. She nodded and turned back to the ME.

"Thanks for your time. If you find anything else please call me," she said, handing him her card and direct dial number. The ME took it and stuffed the slip of paper in his pocket.

"Be careful Megan. This guy is dangerous. He isn't just killing at random; I think there will be a pattern emerging soon." Megan nodded slowly in reply, set her lips tightly together again, then turned and walked for the door.

Once in the car, she pushed the keys into the ignition and started the engine. She sat there looking through the windscreen out at the cold daylight. It was sunny but cool. The rain had been pushed away and replaced with a high pressure system that promised good weather for a few days. It would be a welcome reprieve from the rain.

"What are you thinking?" I ventured.

Megan shook her head and said nothing. I sat in silence waiting for her to say or do something. What she did I didn't expect.

Tears started rolling down her cheeks. She sat in the seat; her head dropped into her hands and she began sobbing. I waited, not sure if it was appropriate to say something or do something. I could understand her frustration, having a murderer with a hard on for you is not something anyone should have to tolerate.

She lifted her head and looked at me, her eyes red, fear lining her lips. Right then I made a promise to myself; I would find this asshole and kill him. Or I would die trying.

CHAPTER 38

J akob pushed the door open to the apartment. It didn't take him long to pick the lock and gain entry, he stepped through the door and locked it again behind himself. Jakob walked through the living room into the bedroom and stared hard at the king-size bed pushed up against the far wall. He knew the man's schedule and he knew that he would be home in an hour.

"More than enough time." He mumbled to himself.

He walked towards the large screen television and touched the power switch. It hummed into life and began playing something from the Sky movies channel. He hit mute and set about changing the channels frequency. He wanted a distraction so he could carry out his elaborate plan.

Jakob glanced at his watch; it was four-thirty in the afternoon. Traffic in the central business district was chaos. It was the only thing about the city Jakob despised; city drivers could be so arrogant.

He pushed a compact disc into the DVD player. He had made it one night during one of the man's explicit encounters with the blonde piece of meat from the restaurant. It was his gift to him and he hoped he would appreciate it. He stood up and stepped back, admiring his handy work then spun a full circle in the bedroom. He had already chosen the closet to hide in. Jakob walked towards it and pulled the door open. He looked at the expensive clothes hanging on the racks and scoffed to himself. Jakob considered himself above such self-gratuitous crap, and outwardly scorned the lower kind of people that indulged. Although he wouldn't admit it to himself, he secretly wished he did own just a few of such soft, well-tailored items.

Jakob checked his watch again, ten minutes had passed.

"Showtime," he mumbled. Jakob stepped into the closet and pulled the door shut.

Tim fought through traffic; every light he caught was red, causing him to wait. His frustration was beginning to swell, and he slammed his fist against the steering wheel, causing the horn to scream in protest.

"COME ON!" he yelled. The person in the car next to him looked across the passenger seat and glared at him. Tim turned and gave the guy the universal "fuck you" sign and waited for the driver to look away. He didn't have to wait long. People in this town were all bravado until they were actually faced, then they usually backed down pretty quick. Especially since he was toned and ripped, his gym time was paying off.

The light turned green, and Tim slammed his foot on the throttle. True to the salesman's spiel, the BMW rocketed across the intersection. He was having second thoughts about his apartment he had bought in the city; it was proving a real pain in the ass to get to at the best of times. But for now, the positives far outweighed the negatives in his eyes. He had girls flocking to meet him and to sleep with him. A smile grew across his lips as he shoved his way into a left-hand turning bay and powered the BMW up Queen Street. He owned one of the most sought-after penthouses in the city and was looking forward to putting his feet up with a margarita. He wanted to watch the video he'd made recently of his time with the bimbo he had met. He knew the video would be good; he had multiple cameras rigged in his apartment for just such an event. His large, and wealthy, following in a particular chat room ensured he would keep the videos coming.

Tim pulled into the private underground garage and swiped a pass card to open the electronic gate. The tires chirped as he drove quickly down the ramp and found his dedicated spot amongst the concrete pillars. He climbed out of the car and slammed the door shut, then touched the alarm button on his key fob. He rode the elevator to the sixth floor and walked towards his entrance.

Tim keyed the door and pushed it open. Inside, he dumped his bag on the kitchen countertop and headed straight for the liquor cabinet. He took his time mixing the perfect margarita then walked into his living room and flicked on the television.

The screen came up blank. Waves of static rippled across the plasma display. Tim frowned, stood up, and went to check the cable connecting it to the satellite dish on the roof. It was still attached. Tim grabbed the remote and flicked to other channels, but they all came up with nothing, just static. Just as he turned away to walk to his desk where he kept the manual for the television, it flicked to another screen. Then the display showed Play in the top right-hand corner. It was a movie. Tim watched intent on seeing on what was going on.

"What the hell," he breathed.

The picture was of a man and a woman having sex. A smile crept across his face as he saw the man slide up the woman's thigh with his tongue. Not bad. The image was shot from a distance, so he couldn't quite make out the features of either the man or the woman. Tim started to relax, enjoying the show, and beginning to think that it may be one of his associates playing a prank on him. It was then that the camera zoomed in and he saw himself buried in the blonde bimbo.

Then the heavy breathing came across the surround sound system.

Tim dropped his glass on the designer carpet. Some sick fuck had recorded him without his knowledge.

"Who the fuck?" he roared. Tim couldn't take his eyes off the screen. He couldn't believe someone could invade his privacy like this. Tim ground his fingertips into the palms of his hands and wondered who the hell it was. But in the end it didn't matter. The piano wire of the garrotte Jakob had fashioned himself from a picture caught him across the throat. The pressure caused his trachea to collapse then the thin wire began to cut into the skin around his neck.

"Did you really think I'd let it go, did you really think you would get away with it, you arrogant piece of shit?" a voice whispered in his ear. Tim struggled to breathe; he could feel himself slipping as the edges of his vision began to blur. Tim reached back and groped for the hands that held the handles. He found a finger and began to yank on it.

Jakob howled in pain as his finger was bent backwards at an insane angle. But he held on tight and kept the pressure on. The man from the street was strong and struggled violently. Jakob moved with him keeping his body behind him and his arms up high. He knew that very soon the fight would disappear and the man would be dead.

Tim kept struggling; his head was fuzzy and beginning to fog. He could feel himself slowing from lack of oxygen, and with one last desperate push he rammed himself backwards towards the bedroom. The pair stumbled through the door, and the pair landed on their backs, with Tim on top of the person trying to kill him. Tim thrust his head back smacking the intruder square in the face. He heard a muffled grunt and felt the wire relax a fraction, before it then tightened up harder than before. Tim's head was wrenched back an excruciating angle. He could see the mirror screwed to the ceiling above his bed and managed to catch a glimpse of the person underneath him.

The last thought he would have was the realisation that it was the man he had accidently walked into over a week earlier.

Chapter 39

My phone chirped and began bouncing its way across the table. I picked it up and glanced at the number. It was Megan.

"There's been another murder," she said when I answered. It was ten o'clock in the evening, and I was intently watching the computer screen in front of me.

"Where?"

"Downtown, Queen Street. Some corporate hotshot failed to turn up to work and his secretary couldn't raise him on the phone. She went around to his apartment and found him dead on the floor."

"OK, I'm coming up. I'll be there in about three-quarters of an hour. Is anyone there now?" I asked.

"Yes. I'm going there now." She told me the address then hung up. I yawned, looked at the time, then grabbed my coat off the back of a chair and headed for the door. It took me less time than I thought it would to get there, traffic was light and there were no accidents on the motorway.

I arrived at the address on Queen Street and parked a few hundred metres down the road. There was traffic but it wasn't very heavy. The police had cordoned off the small but exclusive apartment block.

I walked to the edge of the taped-off area, and stopped to casually remove my phone from a hidden pocket in my jacket. Megan answered after the third ring.

"I'm downstairs, outside the tape," I said by way of greeting. "I'll be right down." Click.

I slipped the phone back in its pocket and waited in the cold. Not my idea of an evening in town. I looked up at the building, then turned and surveyed the surrounding buildings. It was small, a dwarf surrounded by giants, but the outside of the building spoke of money. I guess if someone wanted to be seen to be someone, then this was the place to be seen in. I smiled to myself, there were so many superficial people here it was unbelievable.

I was still looking up at the building when Megan walked up to me. "It's a nice building. Rich people live here." She stated. I kept my eyes on the sixth floor and watched the fluorescent lights flicker and flash in the windows of what I assumed was the victim's apartment.

"The victim's name is Tim Rott. He was a financial investor working in the local office of a multinational company. As I told you on the phone, he failed to show at his office and his secretary came looking for him. He was found lying on the floor of his bedroom. There is a sharp line across his neck." Megan showed me by running her hand from left to right high across her throat. "It looks like he was strangled."

"Does it look like our guy?" I asked.

Megan shrugged her shoulders. "Anything is possible. In fact, Tim is physically quite big, and it looks like he worked out. It would take someone quite strong and tall to kill him that way." Megan looked up at the apartment. I stayed quiet for a long moment.

"Was he gay?" I asked.

Megan turned and looked at me with a doubtful look on her face.

"Do you mean 'could it have been a messy divorce' or something like it?" she asked back.

I nodded. "Maybe he started seeing someone else and his soon-to-be-ex- boyfriend came home and caught him in the act, then, in a fit of rage killed Tim." I suggested. Megan thought about it but I could tell by the look on her face that she wasn't buying it.

"OK, it's plausible but I just can't get there. What if it was an ex-girlfriend? Maybe someone he met at a gym?" she suggested.

"It's possible."

I sighed and looked back at the windows flashing in the night air and asked myself what JR44 possibly stood to gain by killing Tim Rott. It could be anything, money, drugs, or sex. I turned and looked down the street, then back up the other direction. The cordon was tighter than the scene on Great North Road; I guess Captain Holmes wanted to keep the disruption to a minimum.

I again thought that this was getting me nowhere. Every time this asshole showed up and murdered someone, he left us nothing. Unless he slipped up and soon, he could run and we might never catch him. Megan's phone rang and she snatched it from its holder. She opened it and said nothing. I watched her face; the expression didn't change at all during the one-sided conversation. I looked back up at the sixth floor window and could see someone's back pressed against the window. Then the person turned around and looked down at the street.

"OK, we'll be right up." She clicked her phone shut and stuffed it back into its pouch then looked at me.

"What?" I asked.

"We just got a break." She lifted the cordon tape, waited for me to step through then took off at a run for the building.

She tapped her foot impatiently as the lift climbed to the penthouse. It took us all of five seconds to climb the distance but according to Megan's body language, even that was taking far too long. The doors sprung open and she headed for the apartment door at speed. She nodded to the officer standing at the door, and he had opened it for her before she arrived.

We stepped into the apartment; to me it looked like organised chaos. I counted thirty people from various departments scattered around the living room, and a few more I couldn't see in the bedroom. If I ignored all the equipment the police had brought along, the apartment looked very upmarket. A huge widescreen television sat in the very centre of the living room up against the far wall. A surround sound system sat unobtrusively beneath the DVD player. There were speakers embedded flush with the walls, which I guessed were designed to give the feeling that one was in a theatre, as if it were happening right in front of you.

One of the tech guys came up to Megan. He was short and slightly balding, the same guy from the scene on Great North Road. He had rimless glasses perched on the end of his nose, and a white dust coat covering his oversize stomach. He skipped the greeting and launched straight into his findings.

"We have a video of the guy," he said all at once. It sounded like a jumble of words not spoken in order. He was about to start in with an explanation when Megan put her hands on his shoulders and stopped him.

"Marty, stop. Take a deep breath and start again," she said calmly.

Marty stopped and gathered his thoughts for a few seconds, then started again.

"The guy who lives here, Tim, he has the whole placed wired for CCTV." I looked around at the corners of the ceiling but couldn't see anything obvious.

"What do you mean? Is the whole building fitted with surveillance or just this apartment?"

Marty looked at me and I could see a flicker of recognition in his face.

I was getting uncomfortably well-known.

"The whole building is rigged, but the equipment we found here is very high end. The owners of the building would have wanted whoever brought the apartments to feel safe, but they wouldn't have fitted equipment anything like the quality of what we've found here the computer alone for something like this range in the thousands of dollars. Motion activated. Very cool stuff."

Marty paused, looked around at his audience, and when he realised no one was going to interrupt him he carried on.

"But that isn't the interesting part. We powered up the computer and found the memory half full with videos. Some ripped from the net and some made right here in this living room." I looked at Megan then back at Marty but said nothing.

"There are literally thousands of videos on the drive and all the ones we looked at were pornographic. There are shots from above the bed, videos of him and various women on the couch, on the living room floor, everywhere, most in rather compromising positions." A smile started to grow on his face. Megan stopped the smile in its tracks by clearing her throat and asking a question.

"What about the killer Marty, is there a good shot of his face?" she asked.

Marty nodded then turned and walked towards the bedroom. We followed carefully, stepping over electrical leads and forensic people crawling around on the floor. Marty made a beeline for the wardrobe, it was flooded with light. Megan and I walked into the hot lamps of the fluorescent lights and took in the large space. In the corner sat a small desk and on top, with a tech guy hunched over it, was a small laptop computer. He looked up to see Marty staring down at the screen and Megan's head appearing over his shoulder.

Marty motioned for him to get out of the seat; he wanted the glory of showing her what they had found.

He dragged the mouse from the corner of the screen and minimised the page the other guy was looking at. He clicked on a folder icon that was partially obscured, and the screen redrew into a red background with four files on the page to choose from. Marty clicked on the top left and it opened to show a long list of files. They were all AVI files, which to Marty it meant Tim had been a busy boy. He clicked on a random file and it brought up a media player and the video started playing. The image was perfect. The film was only fifteen minutes long.

"It's more than likely it's been edited to be more usable. We found a Web page on his address bar that has been visited a few hundred times in the last six months. When we went further it asked for a login and a password. We hunted around for one but couldn't find anything. Usually if someone thinks they are safe they will write the password down on a piece of paper but this guy didn't. Probably paranoid, and rightly so. Some of this stuff you wouldn't want to be caught with." Marty clicked on another video as he spoke.

Another home movie started. A blonde woman lay on her back and Tim was working his way up her back. Megan watched the screen then put her hand on Marty's shoulder.

"What is the last video of?" she asked.

Marty looked up from the screen. "Oh, yes, right."

He stopped the video and tapped the icon for the file last modified. The date indicated it had been recorded not long ago. It started playing, and the first thing I noticed was the person in the shot. I remembered seeing him somewhere—but couldn't remember where. I closed my eyes and churned back through the memories. Again, that familiarity.

We watched him move from room to room. He knelt down in front of the television screen in the living room and did something to the controls but we couldn't tell what. I turned and looked at the TV against the back wall of the room then back at the computer screen.

"Marty, stop the video there for a moment." I asked.

He hit pause and I moved from the closet into the living room. No one was paying attention to the television, so I walked up to it and touched the power button. It sprung to life but brought up nothing but static. I bent down and stared at it, waiting for something to happen. Nothing.

Megan came and stood beside me and looked down at the screen. "What about the DVD player?" she asked. I looked up at her then touched it off standby. The screen flickered and settled then the play icon appeared boldly in the corner of the screen.

The shot was a panoramic view of a building. A set of lights glowed near the top of the screen as the camera slowly zoomed in. It took a second or two for the shot to come into focus, but it was unmistakable that the person in the shot was Tim and the blonde from the video.

"Well isn't this a development." Marty added.

I stood up quickly and walked to the window. I looked down at the street below me but could see no one walking the sidewalk. I followed a line of windows in the building across the street then returned to the television.

"Marty, rewind it a few seconds."

He looked at me with a confused look then back at Megan. She nodded, so he did as he was asked. He rewound the video until I told him to stop. It was the wide angle shot of the whole building. I stood up and looked out the window again then back at the screen.

"This was filmed from over there." I said pointing towards the building across the street. I moved closer to the window and gazed at the rooms' level to where I stood. There were one or two possibilities. I turned and headed for the door with Megan behind me.

We stepped into the cool night air and walked across the street to the hotel opposite the apartment building. I stepped inside and walked up to the counter. I tapped the small bell on the top and the sound carried like a tuning fork. There was a shuffling in the back office and a man of about fifty emerged around the door frame and walked across the marble floor towards us, his shoes clicking on the floor. I turned and took in his features. He was tall and thin, greying hair slicked back over his oddly shaped head. He rounded the desk and walked up to us; he was dressed in a tuxedo and had an air of arrogance about him. I knew instantly he was going to be a pain in the ass.

"Ah, can I help you?" he asked, addressing me. I stepped to one side and pointed to Megan.

"You can help her," I replied evenly.

Megan looked at me then flashed her badge to him. If he was alarmed, he didn't show it.

"We have reason to believe someone of interest to the police stayed here within the last week. We need to see the registrar of patrons," she asked, not expecting any problems.

"I'm sorry, ma'am, but that is confidential. You will need a search warrant to look through that."

I rolled my eyes at the comment; nothing was going to be easy. Megan looked at the man and took him in.

"No, we don't, and if you insist on being a pompous, arrogant prick, I'll arrest you for obstruction," she said with a sting in her voice.

The man's eyes widened at the threat; he was about to say something back when Megan slammed her fist down on the wooden countertop.

"Register! Now!" she yelled.

I looked at the man. He had his jaw set and was glaring at her. He glanced at me then back at her. The man reached under the counter and brought up an old-fashioned book bound in dark leather and slammed it down hard. It was obvious he wasn't going to be of any help by the way he crossed his arms and stood there.

I stepped forward and spun the book on the polished surface. I opened it to the last page. I didn't know what we were looking for, but I was hoping something would jump out. There were five rooms occupied at the time of the murder. Only five in a hotel this size? Must have been a slow week.

I looked at the man then down at the book and asked, "Were any of these rooms booked as a single?"

When the man didn't answer I glared up at him, may as well give him some attitude right back. He still had his jaw set firmly and wasn't going to say a word. I forced a smile and returned to the book. I would have to do this the slow way.

Megan's phone chirped, and she removed it from her pocket then stepped away from the desk to answer it. I could hear muffled words but mostly silence. She clicked her phone shut and stepped back to my side. She leaned in close and whispered in my ear, I could smell her perfume. The man across the counter was watching us a little too closely, as though he wanted to be included in the information swap. I held his gaze. Megan stepped back, glanced at the man once, then walked for the door. Once the door had closed I returned to the book.

"I'm going to need the keys for these five rooms." I showed him the numbers I wanted, but he didn't move.

"I'm not with the police. So it would be OK for you to help me. I won't tell anyone." I kept my voice low, but he still didn't move.

"OK, I guess I'll just kick the doors down then."

Without giving him a chance to protest I walked quickly towards the bank of elevators and hit the up button. The door chimed and opened, just as I heard the man yell.

"Wait! Wait!" The old man rushed over and stepped in just as the door was closing. He turned and looked at me.

"I will not have you touching anything in this establishment." I nodded and looked down. One of his fists was balled up. Either he had the room keys in his hands or he was getting ready to hit me. I didn't think it was the latter. The door sprung open on the sixth floor.

The elevator let us out at the end of the hallway; all of the rooms were in front of me. I looked at the register again and picked a name at random. It was written down next to room number 471. I walked the length of the hall and stopped outside the door, indicating that this one would be first. The man picked through the keys, obviously put out by having to assist me in such an intrusive act, and slipped the right one into the lock. As he was about to turn it I put my hand on the door and stopped him.

"Is there anyone in there now?" I asked quietly. "No. Why are you whispering?" he asked too loudly.

I rolled my eyes and turned the lock. The door swung open and I could instantly see the fourth floor of the building across the street. I flipped out my phone and walked across the carpet in the darkness as I dialled Megan's number. She answered on the second ring.

"Did he finally give in and help you?" she asked a smile in her voice. I smiled back then said,

"I'll turn the lights on." I turned around and asked the man to turn the light switch on. He lifted his finger and hesitated momentarily then pushed it down. The bulbs sparked to life and I could see Megan waving in the window.

"OK, get out of there and tell him to let no one in there. I want to send a team up there to sweep it."

"OK, I'll come back over."

"Ah best you don't. Marty's been asking questions that I can't really answer."

"I see. My past coming back to haunt me again," I replied.

"Yes he is. Go to my place, I'll get a copy of the latest video and I'll meet you there in half an hour."

I told her I would get something to eat and see her there. The phone clicked off, and I turned to the guy still standing in the doorway.

"I want you to close and lock this room. No one is to get in here until a team from across the road has been through it, OK? That includes housekeeping."

"I can't do that, we have guests arriving in the morning . . ." I stopped him mid whine and told him quite harshly that if he didn't get on-board then he was liable to end up on the bad side of the lady who accompanied me here. He stayed quiet after that and just nodded to my requests.

I walked out the door into the night air and turned for my car parked down the street. As I walked past the building, I looked towards the top floor. The lights had shifted angle and were facing away from the window, though it was still bright enough to flood the room with light.

I shoved my hands into my pockets and walked down the street. I was getting hungry.

Chapter 40

The trip to Megan's didn't take long. I climbed out into the cold air and placed the box of Chinese food on the bonnet. I decided I wasn't going to wait for her and took the lid off the dish. The smell of hot rice and steamed vegetables with chicken floated into my nostrils. Stabbing the fork into pieces of chicken and asparagus, it went down quickly. As I went for another piece, a set of headlights swung around the edge of the street and made their way towards me. I watched cautiously as the car pulled level with me and swung into the driveway on the opposite side.

Megan climbed out and turned to look across the street at me. She waved me over; I pushed the plastic fork into the rice, gathered up the lid, and walked across the road. She fell in beside me and we walked up the garden path to the front door of her house. She looked around, obviously still unsettled by the intrusion then slipped the key into the lock and opened the door.

Inside it was obvious that she had taken steps to ensure that it would never happen again. She quickly walked up to a security pad and punched in her number. The alarm beeped and a light flashed green twice then stayed green. Megan walked towards the kitchen and switched on a light. Thankfully it wasn't bright. I placed the bag on the countertop and searched the cupboards for plates.

As I walked into the living room the sound of the television came on. I walked to the large couch against the wall and placed the plates on a small side stand next to the armrest. I watched Megan push the disk into the player. She stood up and walked back to the couch and sat down next to me. The picture came on and I could hear the faint sound of cars in the back ground. I guessed the camera was set to a wide field of view. We could see the entire building from this vantage point— with front-row seats of Tim Rott's apartment. The video played out again and it zoomed in on Tim and the blonde.

"Does anyone know who the blonde girl is?" I asked.

Megan answered without turning to me. "I've got someone looking into it."

We sat in thoughtful silence. After five minutes I could hear someone's heavy breathing. I turned and looked at Megan who I found looking back at me, then a look of disgust crept over her features. I turned back to the screen and saw the camera had been pushed to its zoom limits. The image was framed perfectly by the border of the screen.Megan hit the pause button and turned to me.

"OK, we know he likes to watch people. We also know he doesn't like women. We also know his name on the Web is JR44." I nodded and took another mouthful of chicken. "We also know he knows what I look like, and more than possibly what you look like."

I stopped chewing a piece of broccoli and looked at her.

"Then it's a better than even guess he knows where I live, which suits me fine."

Megan eyed me then grinned, just a small smirk. She didn't respond. Instead, she hit the play button and the man's heavy breathing resumed.

I watched as I ate and got halfway through my dinner when the camera wobbled and shook violently.

Suddenly I didn't feel so hungry.

Megan ejected the disk and placed it back in its protective cover. She removed another similar cover from her bag and placed the disk in the tray. This time it was an inside view of Rott's apartment. The camera had switched on as soon as the door was opened. A figure walked in and disappeared from shot. Another screen flicked up, and the figure was in the living room. The man looked around the room cautiously then bent down in front of the television screen. He finished what he was doing then walked slowly into the bedroom studying the surrounding walls and ceilings as he went.

He didn't know it but, he had been no further than six feet from one camera when he looked straight at it. The image of his face was perfect, and it was then that I remembered where I had seen him.

I put my plate down and grabbed the remote from Megan. I rewound a few seconds and paused the video on the picture of him looking at the camera.

I scrolled through my memory from day we met in the café. That was the first time. I had walked in and ordered a tea and joined Megan, her sitting at the only table with an empty chair. As I sat down, I remember glancing at the man sitting behind her. He'd quickly brought the paper up in front of his face. I looked back at Megan.

"It's the man I saw at the café. He was sitting right behind you when I walked in."

Megan said nothing, just stared at the screen. Her hand began to quiver, so she curled her legs up and placed them under her thighs.

"OK. So he definitely knows what we both look like and that we know each other. If he sees us as a combined threat . . ." She trailed off. "This is getting too personal." She didn't sound like the cop in charge now. She took a deep breath.

"First thing tomorrow, I am going to search the licensing database, see if anything turns up. Then I'm going to talk to Waters about getting you a temporary pass to work with me on this, that's where it started. He obviously wants to get to me, and he probably sees you as bonus points."

Nice way to make a man feel good, lady. I looked down at my plate and took another bite.

"Would you stay here tonight?" she asked. I hesitated and looked at her. "I can't."

"You can't or won't?"

"I probably shouldn't."

"Why not?"

I shrugged my shoulders not really wanting to give her an explanation. "It would save you having to drive all the way home again. And the couch is quite comfy." She seemed genuine in her offer; I figured I could probably do with having a second set of eyes in the house too. Besides, I was too tired to argue with her.

She crawled off the couch and brought me a blanket and pillow then shut the television down and headed for the stairs to her bedroom, setting her alarm along the way.

"Good night," she said from the bottom of the stairs. I didn't reply. It didn't take long for her to switch the light off.

I lay awake in the darkness, staring at the ceiling in the semi dark. I wondered what JR44's real name was. Twenty minutes later I had had enough of thinking. I closed my eyes and tried to go to sleep. It was then that I heard the creek of the stairs. She had stepped quietly down the stairs, stopping two from the floor. I looked up at her but said nothing. Thankfully by that time my eyes had adjusted to the darkness. She was wearing a white silky slip that stopped halfway down her thighs, and nothing else underneath.

She walked silently towards the couch and bent down to lift the blanket back. She crawled onto the pillows next to me then pulled the blanket back over top. I could feel the strong muscles in her back against my side. Her hands moved around in the darkness and found mine.

Chapter 41

Jakob cradled his hand; he was pretty sure that idiot had broken a bone, or at the very least snapped a cartilage or something. It hurt like hell. He wrapped it in ice and sat down in the small living room of his house. Looking around at the room, it was furnished with cheap but solid furniture. The house was old and cold; it wasn't much to look at, but it did the job he needed. The main selling point was the small lot of ten acres that came with it. It gave him plenty of space to entertain his hobbies.

He had checked on Melanie and given her some food. Not enough to nourish her, no sense wasting good food, but it was enough for her to do the work he wanted. He had found her swaying at a club and she'd been easily taken. One look at her and he'd decided there and then that she was to be his. Not for anything else but to satisfy his needs when there was no other.

Jakob walked to the fridge and spooned some strawberry ice cream into a bowl. He had loved strawberry ice cream ever since he took his first child. She had told him that her mother used shampoo that smelt like strawberries to wash her hair. He nursed his finger and thought back to the rush of feelings he'd felt as the man from the street struggled then died. That man hadn't realised that Jakob had that power; he could stop anyone, anywhere, anytime he wanted.

The realisation of that thought brought a smile to his face then his mind jumped to his future, when he could look at her. Megan. The name rolled off the tongue like honey. She was special. He would treat her like a princess. He would take very good care of her; give her everything she could need. But in exchange for his care and attention, she would have to do exactly as he told her. If she didn't then he would have to discipline her. Jakob hoped she would like the accommodations he had arranged for her.

He smiled to himself, then stood and walked for the door. He was eager to get things just right and that meant Melanie had to be supervised.

As Jakob walked through the fields he wondered if she would possibly marry him willingly. Maybe one day. He shook his head, he knew she could never love him and he could never love her alone. He had too much love to give; it needed to be shared around. He couldn't keep himself for solely one woman. He even thought if things went well he could keep Melanie too. His smile grew wider as he considered that she would probably not survive, let alone measure up to his standards. Even if she did survive, she would only ever be a slave to him. Someone he could fuck whenever he felt the urge. Someone he kept locked up away from the world, no one needed to see her. Jakob walked into the shade below a small stand of trees. He was only minutes from the main highway, and twenty-five minutes from the swamps of the Hauraki plains. This sort of location provided the convenience he had searched long and hard for. Jakob removed some brush and pulled the door back from the ground. It revealed the set of stairs descending into the darkness. Checking that he was still unobserved, he stepped into the darkness and followed the stairs to the bottom. The heavy steel door blocked his way into the cavern. Jakob looked at it then grabbed the rusty handle and pushed it open then closed it behind himself.

He pulled the string hanging from the centre of the ceiling and the cavern was bathed in bright light. He walked to the end cage and lifted the latch. Melanie lay in the far corner, naked and covered in dirt. Jakob had made her remove the limp, dead body of Donna. He had made her stuff the body behind the door in the far corner, a temporary tomb, which led nowhere. Of course now the little girl wouldn't be a problem.

Jakob stepped inside the cage and kicked Melanie in the thigh. "Get up, wench. You have work to do."

Melanie stirred. She lifted her head and looked at the man who had stolen her life. He was standing there, open and begging to be killed, but she didn't have the strength. She couldn't even stand without feeling tired and dizzy let alone fight and kill him. Jakob kicked her again, and she curled into a tighter ball.

"Get up!" he screamed.

Melanie began to sob, but she slowly unfolded herself. She tried to stand. Jakob grew tired of waiting and grabbed her by an arm and lifted her to her feet. Her head fell backwards and she dry retched. There was nothing in her stomach to throw up.

Jakob yanked her up until she was on her toes and gazed into her eyes. "You better clean this place from top to bottom or I swear to god, woman, I'll make you suffer," he whispered to her. Melanie spat in his face then managed a smile.

"There is nothing you can do that will break me," she whispered back. Jakob glared at her and squeezed her arm as hard as his grip would allow. Melanie began to scream thinly, too weak to struggle. Jakob released the pressure once he grew tired of her screaming and looked into her eyes once again.

"Tidy this shithole, you bitch, or the last thing you remember will be the scream from your throat as I cut out your womb," he snarled. Jakob let her go. She dropped to the floor in a heap. Jakob looked down on the pathetic pile and spat on it.

"You'll get some food tomorrow morning and then you have three days to get this place ready. Don't let me come down here and find it isn't." His voice was cold and threatening.

Melanie looked up at him, hate filling her eyes. She wished she could see this man die. Wished she could see him drown in his own blood.

Chapter 42

I woke in the morning. I opened my eyes and looked around the room. It wasn't the room I remembered falling asleep in. The television was gone and replaced with a set of drawers. A wardrobe door was next to it set in the wall. Either side of Megan's bed were a pair of nightstands. These carried photos showing her and two other people. Context suggested parents. I lay in her bed and studied the room; it was sparsely furnished. Knick-knacks were kept to a minimum, like a person who was intent on not being tied down to any one place. I lay still and listened to the house. The sun was beginning to come through the window and shine straight in my face. I kicked the covers back and climbed out of bed.

"There is a towel in the bathroom if you want a shower," her voice echoed up the staircase.

I pulled my jeans on and walked downstairs with my shirt in my hands. Megan was in the small kitchen putting some eggs and bacon onto two plates. She looked at me and smiled.

"Breakfast is ready when you are," she said pointing at the plates. I walked up to her and wrapped my arms around her.

"Thanks," I whispered in her ear. She turned and kissed me, then pointed to a doorway down the hallway.

"Bathroom," she told me. I grinned and let her go.

I stepped under the shower and went through the full routine. Wash hair and body, but no shave. A quick look at her bathroom said it wasn't ready for a male, which I took as a good sign.

I climbed out of the shower, towelled myself off then dressed. The living room smelt of breakfast and coffee. I grabbed the plate off the kitchen counter and sat opposite her at the small table. I dug into the eggs, which tasted good, and sipped the coffee, which I could feel attacking my senses. I looked across the table at her. She was dressed in a man's shirt. And from what I could see, not much else. We sat in silence and ate breakfast; I thought about last night, wanting to say how much I enjoyed it. Just as I opened my mouth to speak, her phone interrupted me. Megan dropped her fork on the plate and grabbed her phone sitting next to her on the table. "Hello?" She paused to listen. Within seconds, her face fell, and I knew they had found another body.

"Where?" she asked. She nodded and told them that she was on her way.

She clicked the phone off and stood up.

"They've found another body. In the swamps on the plains. It looks like he's found himself a favourite dumping ground."

I nodded and quickly finished my breakfast while she got dressed. I pulled my jacket on and stuffed my phone into its pocket. Suddenly a feeling struck me; things were going to go bad today. Megan pushed a Beretta into its holster under her jacket as she walked down the stairs. She buttoned it then glanced at me, said nothing then headed for the door.

The drive south and east was quiet. It was sunny in Auckland for a change, but the weather over the hills was overcast and cold. We ventured down Highway 27, and before long, she swung left on a road that headed almost dead east.

"This is the same road where we found the little girl. Bastard hung her," she said quietly.

The road was dead straight almost to the ranges that ran North-South separating the coastal Bay of Plenty from the flat land of Waikato. She pulled over behind another squad car about halfway down. We climbed out into the cold air and headed towards the constable standing on the side of the road. Megan flashed her badge to him and asked him where the body was.

"Down that path about one hundred and fifty metres, be careful, it's pretty swampy in there and getting worse." He pointed to a small opening in the vegetation.

I walked towards it and stopped. It looked like a natural path that had been forced wider by the passage of people. I pushed my way into the scrub and followed the worn path into the swamp. The path twisted and turned in every direction. I knew it would be very easy to get lost down here.

"How was the body found?" I asked. I could hear Megan squelching through the mud behind me.

"Spotter plane. It was searching for drugs when it saw something lying in the mud. It must have gotten a closer look. Apparently the body is filthy." We walked in silence the rest of the way. The path began to open up and dead-ended in a small hollow. We stopped at what was the entrance to the clearing and looked around. Two cops were standing around talking when we walked up to them. One of the officers recognised Megan and went to meet her.

"Detective," he said nodding at her. "The body is there in the mud. We have kept contamination to a minimum. Also, a team is on the way to remove it when you are ready."

The officer behind him was looking at me out of the corner of his eye. I pretended not to notice and surveyed the body in the mud. If it was spotted from the sky, they must have struck it purely by luck. It was hard enough to see standing right in front of it. I turned to Megan as the officer stepped back to his conversation.

"I don't think they like me," I whispered to her. Megan grinned. "Well, you are a wanted fugitive. Well, sort of. No one knows exactly what you look like. We haven't been able to catch a glimpse of you yet, so I guess they are wondering what you are doing here," she whispered back. I nodded then looked down at the body in the shallow mud pool. The person looked young but I couldn't really tell. The skin was pulled taut over the bones with numerous ragged holes emphasising that the corpse had been out in the elements for a very long time. We waited around for half an hour;

I could feel the officer's eyes on me, asking unheard questions. I casually looked in their direction then back at Megan.

"Excuse me, sir? Who exactly are you?" It was the officer who had been eyeballing me from the beginning. I pointed at Megan, not answering, and kept studying the body in the mud. The officer wasn't going to be brushed off that easily.

"Sir, what is your name?" he asked again this time while walking over to us. Megan stepped between us and answered for me.

"That is none of your business, Sergeant." The officer stopped and looked at me then at Megan.

"This is an official crime scene, and so far I haven't seen an official badge from him. If I am to do my job properly, then I need to see identification." He was pointing at me as he spoke, but looking at Megan. She was about to answer, but I stopped her.

"It's OK," I said as I reached into a jacket pocket and pulled out identification. It was false of course; Megan eyed it then looked at me. It said I was a detective from Australia. My name was Clarke.

"We have had a spate of murders in Sydney, I was sent here to see if there were any similarities. Depending on the details, there's a chance it could be the same person, or more likely a copycat." I explained. The officer eyed me then Megan; the story was pretty thin.

"No one told me that you were here," he complained. This time, Megan stepped in.

"That isn't your concern, Sergeant. Your concern is keeping this crime scene clear—which you have done admirably. If Captain Holmes thought it was necessary for you to know that Mr. Clarke was here, he would have told you himself." The officer stepped back, obviously unhappy about the situation but unable to do anything about it.

We walked back to the road in silence. Once we were turned around and headed back to Auckland, she asked, "So when were you going to tell me about that?" pointing at my jacket. I smirked and said nothing. Sometimes it's better to keep your trap shut.

"You do realise you could get into a lot of trouble if they find out that you showed them false ID." I nodded but still didn't say anything. She stayed silent for five minutes then said,

"We need to talk about last night."

I turned slowly to look at her. I had a feeling this was about to happen. "What's to talk about? We are both grown adults. As far as I am concerned, it was great. But I understand it was a one-off, and I'll leave it at that."

She didn't respond, but she looked she wanted to. She kept her eyes on the road.

"Am I right? It was a one-off, yes?' I asked. She turned to look at me. "I don't know what to think," she confessed.

I stayed quiet for the rest of the trip.

CHAPTER 43

I drove into the tight garage and climbed out of my car. It was late and dark, and I was hungry again. We had visited the morgue to re-cover our tracks, just to make sure we didn't miss anything. But now we had a picture and a video of JR44. Surely it would only be a matter of time before he made a mistake. The trouble was that the more time it took, the longer he was on the streets. I sat down in front of the computer and picked up the phone, then put it down again. I didn't want to involve Dan, but he had the know- how on computers. I picked up the receiver again and dialled his number.

"Yeah," he answered.

I looked down at the picture then spoke. "It's me, I'll keep this short. I'm sending you a picture. I want to know who it is, can you handle that?"

"Hey, Emery, long time no hear! Good to hear from you too," he said in a sing-song voice.

"Dan, yes or no. Can you handle it?" I asked again, impatience creeping into my voice.

"Yes, of course I can. I can do anything for a good cause."

I slipped the picture onto the scanner screen and closed the lid, then woke the computer up and brought the image to the front. I attached it to an e-mail and fired it into the ether. I was still on the phone and heard the chime on Dan's computer telling him he had mail. Dan said nothing as he opened it.

"Kind of looks like a child molester. Or well, you know what society perceives a molester to look like."

"DAN!"

"OK, OK. I'm breaking it down now." I waited in silence for thirty seconds then asked, "How long is this going to take?"

"A while. I'll give you a call back when I find something."

"OK, but don't take too long. And before you ask, yes this means you are on the payroll if we catch him." I hung up the phone before Dan could say anything. I crossed my fingers hoping I didn't have to wait too long. I needed the information now, if there was any to find.

Dan hung up the phone and looked at the picture on the screen in front of him. The man was greying. He had brown eyes with a sparse beard covering his face. First Dan plugged his software into the drivers licensing system. If this man had a licence, then the system would tell him about it. The computer screen dulled, and a large hourglass appeared. It tumbled end over end, pouring the digital sand from one end to the other.

Dan waited ten minutes, the frown growing on his face. It usually only took this long if the picture was either not found or blocked for some reason. Another thirty seconds later, the computer told him no person existed, at least according to the land transport agency. He closed the connection and opened a facial recognition program. He loaded the picture. He removed the beard and a few of the wrinkles, generally tidying the image.

He opened a search program that piggybacked the police and immigration networks and loaded the photo for a search. The program would search every database the police and customs had access to. He hit Enter to start the process then sat back. He watched the screen dull and the hourglass icon appear again. Dan glanced at the clock on the wall; it had been twenty minutes since Emery had called, and he had been searching for most of it. He was confident his firewall would keep him hidden, but he was taking a huge risk with the length of time he was inside the police network. If one of them happened to stumble upon him then—he shuddered. It wasn't worth thinking about.

The computer beeped and stopped suddenly, filling the screen with information. They were newspaper articles. Dan read the first; it stated that two girls had been found dead in a grove of trees in a park many years ago. It was located in a small town in the Waikato area. A boy matching the description of the man in the photo, although a lot younger, was seen leaving the trees and heading towards town. A woman went to investigate and found the two girls naked, tied together with their own clothes. Both were dead.

The police would never lay it at the boy's feet. After reading the rest of the article, Dan scrolled through a rap sheet. There were a few minor incidents, but nothing what he would call "bad". If one cared to check, they would find he had a small list of minor acts he had done himself. But no one would find it though, his junior record was still in the police system, but clean slate legislation would generally stop anyone from going to look for it. And even then, they'd still need a point in the right direction. The sheet indicated violence and misbehaviour, but nothing sinister.

Dan read through the sheet, jotting things down on a scribble pad. At the top he wrote the name he'd managed to dig up. Jakob Richardson. JR44. He got on the phone.

It was close to midnight when my computer chimed and the phone rang at the same time. I had a shower and something to eat and was restlessly pacing around the living room in my house. I had thoughts of Megan and this JR44 revolving through my head. Every now and then, I would contemplate a safe, quiet, steady life. Get away from the danger. I didn't contemplate it long. This wasn't a life I was ready to give up yet.

I yanked the phone off the cradle. "Well?"

"Well, what?" Megan asked.

"Oh sorry, I thought you were someone else. I was kind of expecting a phone call," I said as I sat down at my computer and touched the mouse. I clicked the mail icon and opened the unread folder. A new e-mail from Dan had arrived. I looked at the clock; it had taken him an hour to find anything, and what he found wasn't very much. There were only a few articles, so I made short work of reading them.

"Are you still there?" Megan asked.

"Huh, yeah, sorry. Can I call you back later? I'm kind of in the middle of something." I asked, though not really wanting to break off the call.

"Um, sure." She hung up without saying good-bye.

I dropped the phone back on the table and looked at it. I didn't like how that sounded. I spent thirty minutes going over what Dan had sent to me. It didn't really tell me anything useful other than his name. There was some indication he had disappeared recently, or gone into hiding. I was about to pick up the phone again when it started ringing. I answered it.

"Dan! I have some more information."

"I'm glad to hear you are taking such an interest in me, Emery. Yes, I know who you are and what you look like to. Oh, and Megan, isn't she a little peach, I'm definitely looking forward to meeting her and consummating our relationship together."

"You sick…!" I spat into the phone. He cut me off.

"Now, now, Emery. You shouldn't get wound up. It won't do anyone any good, especially Megan," he taunted. Then he started to cackle. The laugh almost pushed me over the top.

"When I find you, I'm going to rip your spine out, I swear," I gnashed.

"You are going to do no such thing, Emery. Instead you are going to bring Megan to me. And I know you will, because if you don't, I'll kill your young friend here. Isn't that right, Dan?"

I heard a heavy punch then what sounded like a body thudding to the floor.

"I'll be in touch." He laughed then the line went dead.

Chapter 44

. . . .

Jakob looked down at the pathetic pile of human waste on the floor.

"You shouldn't have met with him, Dan, he's a bad influence. I, however, will allow you to change your ways," Jakob said.

Dan lay on the floor. His head swam as bolts of pain ripped across his eyes. Spots were exploding in front of him. The back of his head was on fire. Jakob dropped the bat on the floor next to Dan's head. He grabbed a roll of tape and tied his hands behind his back. He then tore off a piece and slapped it across his lips.

"There, picture perfect," Jakob said, looking down at him. He bent down and grabbed Dan by the scruff and lifted him almost off the ground. Pain flashed through Dan's head, and he screwed his eyes shut, trying to fight off the fresh wave of nausea that hit him. He wasn't sure what had happened—he recalled that he was about to call Emery then . . . nothing. It was like that space in his memory didn't exist. He'd woken lying on the floor with someone standing over him. His computer lay broken on the floor; its screen had a huge hole punched through it. In pain, he rolled over. That was when he saw the person holding a baseball bat.

Jakob marched, pushed Dan towards the door. He had no use for him, other than serving as bait. Once outside, he shoved Dan into his van. The windows were tinted almost to the point of being completely black. Jakob slammed the door shut and ran around to the front and climbed into the driver's seat. He keyed the ignition and roared out of the driveway. Dan tried to sit up, but waves of nausea kept hitting him and folding him in half. He passed out twice more, and each time he woke, they were still moving. He had no idea how long he had been unconscious, or how far he'd travelled.

It took Jakob only twenty minutes to cover the distance to his small plot of land from where he had ambushed Dan in the Bombay hills. Jakob had said nothing to him as he drove but did watch him carefully in the mirror. He had passed out a couple of times. Jakob smiled to himself; he was getting his technique right and had almost honed it to a fine art. He thought about the coming hours; it was going to be a dangerous time for him, but he knew he would come through it. And then he would finally be with her.

Jakob smacked the steering wheel as he jumped out of his seat with excitement. He looked back at Dan with elation on his face. He turned back and nearly missed a gentle curve in the road. The van swerved wildly on the gravel in the darkness, throwing Dan against the opposite wall, knocking him unconscious again. Jakob regained control then turned and looked over the seat again.

"Sorry about that." He laughed.

Jakob put his foot down harder, pushing the van near to its limits of speed and control. He had just left Maramarua Township behind when he slowed violently and turned down a bumpy gravel road. He followed it to its conclusion and bumped over a cattle stop onto his property. Dan stirred in the back and Jakob turned to look at him.

"Home sweet home," he said with a grin. Jakob turned back to the front and concentrated on driving towards the very rear of the property where it backed on to the hills and to the grove of trees. He climbed a small rise and manoeuvred the van slowly through the trees. He stopped and climbed out, leaving the engine running and the headlights on so he could see. Not that he needed them. Jakob could navigate here in the dark. He reached the marked tree then reached down and grabbed a thick chain welded to another steel door. An additional measure of security he had installed to placate his paranoia. It was an effort for him to move it, so he wasn't worried about his guests escaping. The door slammed open in a cloud of invisible dust. Jakob reached in and touched a hidden light switch, and a small row of lights cast a dull glow on the stairs to the steel door waiting at the landing. Jakob turned and walked quickly back to the van. Throwing open the rear doors, he found Dan still unconscious on the floor, a small trickle of blood running from his nose. Jakob grabbed his shirt, bunching it in his fist then yanked the inert body out of the van to land on the ground with a thump. Jakob dragged him to the entrance, and then, without a care, hefted him down the stairs to the cavern below. He stepped over the crumpled heap and placed his shoulder against the heavy steel door then pushed. It squealed as it opened slowly. He peered into the darkness, but couldn't see Melanie. Jakob bunched Dan's shirt in his fist and stepped into the black, groping around for the string hanging from the ceiling. He found it and pulled it quickly, illuminating the cavern.

Melanie sat in the corner of a cage. She hadn't moved for twelve whole hours, and she doubted she would have been able to even if she wanted to. The cavern which had been her prison for as long as she could remember was still exactly as it was when he left. She watched cautiously as Jakob stomped in, dragging another body behind him. He walked up to another cage and threw the limp body inside then locked it with a padlock. Jakob looked down at the man lying on the floor and sneered.

"Don't worry. I'm sure soon he will be here to rescue you." Dan's headed rolled back, and his eyes flickered open momentarily then shut again. Jakob stepped towards Melanie's cage, the door still hung open. She lifted her head slowly and gazed at the man standing before her.

"Why is this place still a filthy mess?" he asked casually. Melanie didn't answer. Jakob grabbed the door and slammed it shut then locked it.

"You had a chance, now you have lost it," he said as he dropped the padlock against the steel. Jakob walked to the door and closed it behind himself leaving the light on. With a resounding final boom, he dropped the top door into place and headed for the van again. He threw it into reverse and backed slowly out of the trees and headed for the highway again. Jakob was thinking that if he played his cards right, he wouldn't have to travel far to find Megan; in fact, she would almost be brought to him.

CHAPTER 45

I slammed the phone down; he had gotten to Dan. It bounced on the desk and clattered to the floor. I knew what he would do next; he was going after Megan. I picked up the phone and plugged it back into the wall then furiously dialled her number. She answered after the third ring.

"You do realise that its one o'clock in the morning, Emery?" She sounded groggy.

"Get out of bed and get dressed. He's coming for you right now!" I blurted into the phone.

"What, who, you mean JR44 is coming here, now?" she asked, alarm in her voice.

"Yes, right now, and the asshole's name is Jakob Richardson. Get dressed and get out of there," I yelled down the phone.

"No, I'm going to stay," she replied. I could hear the stubbornness in her voice.

"Megan, you can't do this alone. He knows where you live, and he knows there aren't any cops there. He has already got to another contact of mine as I was talking to him on the phone," I explained. I waited for her to say something then heard her sigh.

"OK, does he know where you live?" she asked.

"Not that I'm aware of, but it has to be safer than your place right now." I gave her my address and told her to be here as soon as she could. I put the phone down and walked quickly to my bedroom. I pulled the Beretta from its holster then screwed on a silencer. I didn't want it to turn into an all-out war in the middle of the small town I lived in. No point scaring the locals. Jakob hit the intersection that joined the state highway to the expressway and ran all the way to Auckland. He didn't turn right though, instead he turned left and headed south towards Hamilton. After ten minutes travelling, he stopped at a service station on the side of the expressway and found a public payphone. He dialled a number he had committed to memory and waited for someone to answer. Even though it was near two o'clock in the morning, he knew someone would be there. It was answered after the fifth ring. Jakob was greeted by a tired voice, obviously someone pulling double shifts trying to impress the boss.

"Hello." This was said as if it was a cursory feature, as if it needed to be said but he didn't really mean it.

"Uh yes, I'd like to report a kidnapping," Jakob said in a spritely voice. He heard a shuffle on the other end then the voice came through loud and clear.

"A kidnapping? Where was this, sir?" the person on the other end asked.

Jakob gave him Emery's address and a few sketchy details.

"Sir, if this is an emergency, you should call 111. This is only a direct line to Captain Holmes's office."

"I am aware of that, but Captain Holmes told me I could call him anytime, day or night," he pleaded.

"OK. Yes, all right, I'll get right on it. And what was your name, sir?" the man on the other end asked.

"I'm just a concerned citizen." Then Jakob hung up the phone.

Megan slammed the door of her car and gunned the engine for the motorway. It was going to take her close to an hour for her to get to Emery's. She had a map of the Waikato district and found it sitting off the highway by two kilometres, nestled in a valley. She had never been there before but had driven past the turnoff sign plenty of times. The road between Hamilton and Auckland at one time ran through the township, but now with the remapping of the roads, the new expressway had been moved to the west.

She pushed nearly a 160 kilometres an hour down the southern motorway, hoping there were no police or speed traps hiding along the way. She had left without locking her house, the realisation dawning on her once she hit the motorway. In hindsight she thought she should have turned around, but being back at the house alone was probably a bad idea. She had thrown some clothes on and grabbed only her gun and jacket before she had left the house at a sprint.

This was all happening too fast. They had only just days ago managed to find a picture of Jakob and now he was coming for her. She could feel panic beginning to creep in but fought it back and told herself to stop being stupid.

Mercer service centre passed by in a flash, and finally the floodlights on the sides of the road disappeared. She plunged into darkness with only the two beams from her car lighting the road in front of her. Megan pushed her foot down harder and watched her speed climb to dangerous levels. She hit the turnoff in record time and gunned the car up and over the hill towards the township. The car bumped over the train tracks, and she passed through the main part of town. She looked at all the shops; everything was locked up tight. Megan found the driveway and turned down it. The car skidded to a halt on the gravel outside just as Emery stepped out carrying a pistol.

Jakob tailed Megan from a safe distance, but he had to push the large van just to keep her in sight. He looked down at the speedometer and whistled.

"Talk about double standards." He mumbled to himself.

Jakob followed her into the small township and parked his van between two street lamps on the main road. He opened the door slowly, grabbed a shoulder bag, and slipped it over his shoulders. He ran to where he saw her turn and walked slowly in the shadows until he found a house with lights on. Jakob figured that it being near three in the morning that not many people would be awake, and the chances of finding Megan and Emery this way would be good.

He peered down a long driveway and saw the familiar outline of the car he had been chasing from Mercer. As he had predicted, they played straight into his hands. Jakob checked his watch; it was ten to three. He figured the police would take around thirty minutes to get here from the next town, so he had to work fast. Jakob walked down the long gravel drive towards the low-lying brick house. Where the driveway opened out into the carport off to the right, there was a gap between the wall and the fence that ran behind it. He followed it around and waited by a door where he could hear their conversation clearly.

Megan stepped inside. The floor was a dark hardwood, and the various pictures hanging stood stark against the white walls. An old but sturdy table sat in the middle of the dining room. In one corner was a fireplace, and opposite that was a small desk with a computer screen perched on top. Up two steps were a small kitchen and a hallway leading down to the rear of the house. Megan dropped her gun on the table and turned to Emery.

"This isn't necessary, really. I can take care of myself, Emery," she said, trying to play it down. I looked her up and down.

"If it isn't necessary, why is your hand shaking?" I pointed. She looked down then quickly stuffed her hands into her jeans pockets. I looked her in the eye and stepped close to her.

"Have you called the police yet?" I asked. She shook her head. "Don't you think that would be a wise idea?"

Megan opened her mouth then closed it again. It took her several more seconds to answer.

"It's hard for me. I mean, it's hard for a woman, particularly in the force. They either look at you as someone who is out to prove something or someone who has an axe to grind. And before you say anything," she finished before I could say anything, "I am aware that this is not the ideal situation to prove to them who I am."

I looked at her for a second longer then walked into the kitchen and pressed the switch for the kettle. I walked to my room and put the Beretta on the dressing table then returned to make a coffee. I stood at the bench and waited for the water to boil. The kettle clicked and died. I poured the water into the coffee then stirred it slowly and began thinking how this was going to end. I turned and lifted the cup then placed it gently on the living room table and pointed through the dining room to a spare room.

"The bed is made. I suggest you call Holmes and tell him where you are and what is going on."

Megan looked at me, I couldn't read her expression.

"Fine." She took her cup and gun towards the room and left me standing in the living room. I didn't follow her. Instead I walked down the hallway to my room and fell onto the bed, too tired to take even my shoes off.

Jakob heard the limited conversation. It made his blood boil that Emery could treat her in such a way. He would never do that to her. When she joined him, he would treat her with respect, but she would still have to do what he told her to do, otherwise . . .

The thought trailed off, and a smile crept over his face. Jakob looked at his watch. He had been listening and waiting for ten minutes; he had to act soon or the place would be overrun with cops. Jakob reached into his bag and carefully lifted a grenade from its depths. He looked at it and clenched it in his fist; Emery was about to pay for his sins. Slowly he crept from his hiding place and walked silently around to the front door. He stopped and carefully placed the grenade in his pocket and removed a set of lock picks then stepped over the low hedge.

Jakob slowly worked a lock pick into the keyhole and turned the lock.

It was now or never.

Jakob yanked the door open and stepped into the living room then looked towards the spare room as he pulled the pin from the grenade and began to laugh.

I sat bolt upright in bed. The laugh echoed down the hall followed by a metallic thud. I leapt from the covers and picked up my Beretta and ran to the door to peer down the hallway. Jakob was standing in the doorway, backlit by ambient street light. He pointed and laughed at me. I looked down slowly and saw the grenade between my feet and dived sideways and rolled into the bathroom behind the door.

Chapter 46

The explosion knocks me to the floor. Wood splinters and chunks of drywall land on me, filling my lungs with choking dust. This isn't what I have planned. Everything has turned to shit in a matter of seconds.

"You'll never get her back, Emery!" a voice yells from the other end of the house.

I lift my head slowly, lights flickering on and off randomly. The back of my head feels as if it's on fire. I reach back slowly to touch it and feel something warm and sticky.

"Fuck," I mumble.

"Wrong place, wrong time yet again, Emery!"

Lifting myself up on to my hands and knees, my head swims with darkness, and I instantly feel dizzy. My head throbs violently as I search the chaos on the floor for my gun. The lights flick off again, and I fall into darkness. All I can hear is my breathing. Then another noise comes through the night, the sound of sirens screaming.

"God damn it." My hand knocks against something metal, and I grope for it.

"Here comes the cavalry, Emery, might not be safe here for any of us!"

The something metal turns out to be my pistol. I pull the slide back and let it slam home again. Thankfully, the suppressor is still attached to the muzzle. That's some comfort—I'd thought for a second that the grenade had ruined my chances. The lights begin to flicker again and I can see more clearly, the dust has settled somewhat. I rise to my feet and look into what's left of the mirror hanging on the wall over the sink. In the sputtering, I can see my face is covered in blood and plaster, looking like something out of a horror movie. No time for vanity now. I push the pistol out in front of me and move slowly towards the door. I can't lose her, mustn't lose her. If I don't get her back, I know she will die.

"What's wrong? You scared of the feds?" I yell back. I hear nothing for a short moment and then I hear it again. The laughter. That cackle belongs to the jerk-off that has been taunting the police, and me, for several months. His type of cat and mouse games means innocent people were getting caught in the cross fire.

"Don't worry, Emery, I'll take extra good care of her! Extra special care!" I can almost see the grin on his face as he says it, making my skin crawl. I have seen enough of what this mutt's idea of "special care" is, and what he has done to the girls he'd kidnapped was far from human.

"Just let her go, it's me you want! Slowly I ease around the doorframe. Looking down the long hallway towards the voice, there is no immediate indication of where he's hiding. The lights flick off again, and I hear a muffled cry.

"No, Emery, that's not how the game is played. You know that."

My vision blurs momentarily then swims back into focus. Looking the other direction down the hallway, I can see lights approaching fast.

"Time for us to leave, Emery. Sorry I can't stay for the reunion but y'know, you have my best wishes." The voice stated in a taunting tone. This mutt really thinks he has everyone under control.

I hear a window smash from a room or two away, followed by another muffled scream. The next sound is something that I had heard before and immediately makes my blood run cold. Something hit the instep of my boot. Something hard. I only had a split second to react. I leap for an open doorway and slam it shut as I roll through it.

The explosion blows the door inwards, ripping it off its hinges and slamming it against the far wall of the bedroom. A slightly different course could have been bad news for me, but thankfully, most of the blast has been absorbed by the door. I stand up quickly, my ears still ringing from the concussion. The end of the hallway is scattered with light.

"Not good. Definitely not good."

I leave the smoking ruins behind and stumble into the night.

Chapter 47

Jakob stepped out into the dark night. He was on edge. Everything had gone right so far. He had researched her as far as he could but her being in a relationship with that pain-in-the-ass Emery had come out of nowhere. The lights and sirens screamed down the street towards them as he dragged Megan towards a break in the fence.

"Get up, bitch!" he snarled as she stumbled. He crushed his fingers into her hair and lifted her off the ground. Megan screamed at the sudden jab of pain running through her skin. Jakob glanced around wildly. He couldn't see Emery anywhere. He was hoping that the last grenade he threw had taken care of him. But he doubted it.

"Come on, move. We have a lot of ground to cover and not a lot of time to do it in." He dragged her forward and forced her into a neighbouring property. The dewy grass made progress slippery, but they were soon standing on the side of the road running parallel to Emery's. He looked down the street and saw no flashing lights. It had been a risk leaving his vehicle parked so close, but he really had no choice. The distance he'd had to cover required a vehicle; otherwise he would have gladly disappeared on foot. He ran along the side of the road, dragging the cop behind him. He pulled the unlocked door open then shoved her inside. Megan turned and kicked out, but Jakob was too quick. He caught her ankle and twisted it sharply to the left. A sharp snap sounded and he felt something give way in her foot. Megan screamed and rocked back in the rear seat. Jakob slammed the door and ran for the driver's side. He started the van and moved down the road, the van's engine roaring in protest. He kept his head lights off until he was well on to State Highway 1 and heading back towards Auckland.

"What the fuck are you doing here?" He was in a rage. He punched the steering wheel, causing the horn to scream in protest. When he received no answer, he repeated himself. "I said, what the fuck you are doing at Emery's house!"

Megan ignored him and concentrated on the pain emanating from her ankle. He had broken it like a twig. Snapped the cartilage with a single twist. She could feel the rage radiating from him in waves.

"If you do not answer me, life for you will get a hell of a lot more painful, Megan. Now answer the fucking question! What are you doing here?"

Megan looked up at Jakob. "Nothing."

Jakob turned and looked back at her with a disgusted look. "Bullshit. You've been banging Emery. I'd know that bastard anywhere. Thinks he's so tough, running around knocking off people like me. Well, you know what; he's not going to find you, ever. Not until I carve you up and post you back to him in pieces." He was spitting as he turned around to yell at her. The vehicle ducked and swerved wildly on the highway. Megan bit down on her lip as her foot slipped off the side of the seat. His tone told her that he was deadly serious and that she was in a lot of trouble.

CHAPTER 48

I climbed to the top of the small hill and watched Jakob stuff Megan into a van. He yelled something I couldn't hear past the ringing in my ears then a scream echoed out of the darkness. My vision slipped momentarily, and the van began to move.

"Ok, this is bad," I breathed. The noise of the sirens slowly cut through the ringing and I saw house lights around the neighbourhood begin to flick on. I looked up and down the road in a daze and saw a car parked on the side. I stumbled over to it and smashed the window with the butt of the Beretta. Inside I found the ignition wires and brought the engine to life. Misspent youth.

I pulled the transmission into drive and slammed my foot on the accelerator. The car rocketed forward, slamming me back in the seat, and my vision blurred dangerously again. The town flew past in a kaleidoscope of street lights. I barely noticed as I concentrated hard on keeping the car on the road and catching the son of a bitch. It wasn't long before I was breaking the speed limit by an excessive margin and had caught what I thought was the van. I had passed no other cars on the way north towards Auckland and decided to hang back. I dipped the lights and kept my distance; blood trickled down my back, and soon, my shirt was sticking to my back. I followed the dark van for what seemed like hours, but a glance at the dashboard told me that in reality it was only thirty minutes.

It turned off the motorway and headed east towards Thames. He wasn't hard to follow as the idiot slowed down. My guess was that he didn't want to be pulled over for speeding by a lone cop on the road. He drove past Maramarua and on into the countryside. I kept pace and at the same time tried to find a cell phone or something I could use to call the police. It wasn't long before Jakob swung off the main highway and turned left down a gravel road. I slowed and watched the van drive faster than was necessary down the road and disappear from view. Slowly I climbed out and looked at the road sign; it said no exit. I grinned; the bastard had backed himself into a corner.

"Got you," I whispered as I climbed back into the car I had commandeered. .

Jakob bumped down the gravel road and hit the cattle stop faster than he should have. Megan screamed in pain as her leg tapped the side of the seat. Jakob looked back over the driver's seat and grinned.

"Don't worry, you will soon have all the comforts of home, darling." He turned his attention back to the track and drove straight towards the grove of trees. Jakob was starting to feel tired. The adrenaline was beginning to wear off, and he'd need to sleep soon. He could think nothing but good thoughts; he had who he wanted, and now it was his time to show her who he could be.

"That bastard Emery will never get her back or treat her like a plaything again,' he thought to himself.

His mind flicked back to Emery's home; he had wrecked it substantially, and hoped like hell that he was having a nice long talk to the police as to the whereabouts of Megan. He knew it couldn't have happened to a nicer person.

Slowly Jakob negotiated the track to the grove of trees and pulled the van to a stop. He cut the engine and climbed out then flicked on a small flashlight. He made his way to the rear door and opened it. Megan lay on the floor and looked up at him in pain. Jakob felt a twinge of guilt about what he had done, but he rationalized it away. He had to have her, and he only did what was necessary. He slowly gathered her up in his arms and put her gently down on the lumpy ground. Megan wailed in pain as the bones in her ankle grated together.

"You will have to stop that, Megan, we don't want to attract any attention," Jakob said looking down at her in a fatherly way. He slammed the door shut and strode the short distance to the heavy steel door with the chain. He shone the light back at Megan to check she was still there then reached down and grabbed a handful of chain and lifted the door back. It slammed to the ground with a resounding thud. He reached down, turned the lights on then headed back to the van. Jakob looked down on Megan and smiled.

"You don't know how long I have waited for this moment. Allow me to formally introduce myself, I'm Jakob Richardson," he said extending his hand. Megan looked up at him and said nothing. She didn't grab his hand, only held his gaze, wanting to kill him. Jakob dropped his arm to his side when he realised that she wasn't about to return the gesture.

He squatted down and brought his face to within inches of her nose and whispered, "If you don't go along, Megan, your expected lifespan will be very short, very short indeed." His hands shot underneath her and lifted her off the ground again as if she weighted nothing. The killer then turned and walked for the entrance to the cavern.

Chapter 49

I drove a short distance down the gravel road then stopped and killed the lights and engine. I stepped out into the night and listened, nothing, no sound, only the ticking of the exhaust as it cooled. I stuffed the Beretta into the waistband of my jeans and started quietly down the road. I could see two sets of lights in the distance and kept my eyes on them as I walked. The first driveway I approached on my right led to a brick house. There were lights on in the front of the house, but I couldn't see anyone moving about. I looked down the track towards the second and only other house on the road and came to a decision. I had to know whether she was here; if she wasn't, then I would have to carry on. It wasn't a situation I was looking forward to. I felt tired and sluggish. The gash on the back of my head had slowed to a seep, but it still hurt like hell.

I slowly walked up the driveway sticking to the grass sides. Nearing the house, I stopped and pulled the pistol out and gently pulled the slide back to chamber a round and flicked the safety off. Holding the pistol low, I moved from shadow to shadow towards a window where I would hopefully see if anyone was inside. My head began to spin and

I dropped to one knee to steady myself. Looking around, I realised that I was out in the open. I crouched and ran quickly to the house then slowly looked inside at an old man lying on a couch watching something on television. This wasn't the place.

I backed away, retreating down the driveway quickly. I stopped in the middle of the road. I listened again and could faintly hear the sound of traffic from the highway over the ringing in my ears. Glancing at my watch, I figured it was going to be sunrise in an hour. It would make my job easier, I thought, but if I waited—I stopped that thought in its tracks.

Jakob walked slowly down the stairs with Megan in his arms. Her broken ankle clipped the wall, and her scream shattered the silence. Jakob stopped at the bottom of the stairs and looked down at her.

"Do that again and I'll cut out your tongue," he said quietly but firmly. Without saying another word, he put his shoulder against the door and pushed. It creaked open, and he gazed into the darkness.

"I hope for your sake, Melanie, this place is ready," he said as he squeezed through the gap. Megan's ankle hit the side of the steel frame, and a small yelp escaped her throat before she was able to clamp her jaws shut. Jakob ignored her and walked slowly into the darkness. He found the string hanging from the ceiling and grabbed it awkwardly as he tried to hold Megan. She slipped from his arms and landed heavily on the floor; this time, she couldn't hold back the scream. The lights came on, and Jakob saw Melanie sitting bolt upright in the far corner of her cage, her eyes wide with shock.

"Melanie, this is Megan, Megan, Melanie. And the waste of space in the other cage is not important." Jacob stated with a flick of his hand.

Megan groaned on the floor. Pain flooded from her ankle and worked its way up to join the pain in her scalp. Her temples were throbbing. Jakob grabbed her by the hair again and pulled her to an empty cage; he swung the door back and dragged her inside before dropping her. Megan bit her lip as a fresh wave of pain sent stars shooting to her eyes.

The walk along the gravel road was slow; as I approached the second house, I looked towards the horizon and saw the faint colour of dawn creeping into the sky. I was going to lose the only advantage I had if I didn't get moving. I moved as quickly as I could along the driveway towards the second house with small lights spaced evenly along its entire length, not what I needed. I stopped and studied the dark form of the house nestled in amongst a ring of trees. I couldn't see any lights or any vehicles. My mind screamed that this was the right place. Creeping slowly and staying as hidden as I could, I approached the house. It looked and felt cold, like no one had been occupying it for some time. Still I had to make sure. I made a circuit around the house, staying in the shadows all the time becoming more and more aware of the lightening horizon.

"She isn't here," I whispered to myself. I realised the time for quiet had passed. Breaking from the shadows, I ran down the driveway onto the gravel road again and slid to a stop then cast my gaze towards the hills. Five hundred metres ahead the, road dead-ended at a cattle stop. I looked up at the horizon and saw a brilliant pink in the gathering clouds. Dawn was coming.

I cleared the cattle stop at a sprint then skidded to a stop. I felt light headed and dizzy and reached back to feel the stinging cut on my head.

All I could feel was caked dried blood; at least it had stopped bleeding. I walked quickly up the track; it snaked up to and disappeared into the hills. And that was when I heard it, an agonising scream breaking the peaceful silence. I stopped and scanned the surrounding grassland and trees. As quick as it had happened, it disappeared. It was still too dark to see, but she was here.

Jakob came back from a low bench brandishing a small knife covered in rust. He stepped into the cage with his new guest and squatted down in front of her.

"See this?" he asked. Megan said nothing as she glanced from the blade to him.

"This was the first thing I used, the first tool of my trade. Though it may not look like much, I can guarantee you it is still as sharp as the first time I used it." He rose to his feet and walked out of the cage and back to the table. He held the knife in one hand and then picked up another object. Megan couldn't make out what it was.

"I don't need a lot to be effective. If you look at most of the others, they have all sorts of instruments." He shook his head as he turned around, a grin on his face.

"I don't need that," he said reassuringly. With a snap of his wrist, the blades on the pear-shaped object Jakob was holding sprung out a quarter inch. Megan eyed the device in horror.

"Would you like me to show you how it works?" He paused. "Or would you like to experience it first hand?" Her throat worked, then she glanced at Melanie. Jakob swung his gaze at the emaciated wretch on the floor of the cage next to her.

"OK, I'll show you." His eyes blazed as he stepped into the cage with Megan. She began to back up as far as she could, but it was no use. Jakob was on top of her before she could defend herself. He drove his knee into her stomach, knocking the wind from her and pinned her to the dirt floor. She struggled, and almost caught him off balance. In steadying himself, he drove the knife into her shoulder and she went rigid with pain. A choked scream echoed around the walls of the small cavern. Jakob snapped his wrist in the opposite direction and brought the pear shaped object in front of her eyes.

"Now lie still, Megan, or this will hurt more than is really necessary." He grinned.

I saw the van in the distance and ran for it, the pistol in both hands in front of me. As I approached it I slowed and kept my eyes on the rear. No one was in it. I looked around in frustration. It was then that I spotted the opening in the ground. I headed for it and as I got closer, I saw the lights leading down below. No wonder he'd gotten away with it for so long. He had carved the steps out of the earth so I took them cautiously. As I reached the bottom, I saw another door and could hear someone talking. The earthen hole smelt dank and full of fear. I reached the second door as silently as I could and peered carefully around the edge. What I saw made my skin crawl.

There were three cages. Jakob was kneeled over Megan in the first, pinning her to the dirt floor. He had something stuck in her shoulder and was busy trying to rip her jeans from her with his free hand. Next to him lay something that I didn't want to even imagine a use for, but it was enough to start all sorts of horror scenes playing in my head.

Next to them in another cage was another girl who looked dead but I couldn't tell for sure. She was lying on the floor, not moving. The end cage held Dan. He was lying on the floor, his eyes open but not moving a muscle.

I pushed around the heavy steel door; Jakob had his left knee driven into her stomach, his right leg extended. The girl on the floor saw me and I raised my finger to my lips hoping she would be quiet. I stepped through the door and silently walked up behind him, it felt like I had been pursuing him for an eternity. Manoeuvring myself so I had a clear shot, I brought the pistol up and took aim at the back of his knee then gently squeezed the trigger.

Jakob tried in vain to push the jeans down Megan's legs. She was struggling but couldn't move with his weight on top of her. A scream began to escape her and she clawed at him when he fell sideways howling in pain. She blinked then turned her head to the left and saw the girl lying on the floor in the next cage, a small smile on her face. His howl echoed around the cave. Turning her head towards the door, she saw Emery, bloodied and bruised, looking down the barrel of a pistol at Jakob.

I moved quickly, stepping into the cage I kicked at Jakob's knee then placed the heel of my boot on it and pressed down. He screamed and rocked backwards as I lunged for Megan and grabbed a handful of her shirt. I dragged her out of the cage, turned then shot Jakob through his remaining good knee. He screamed once again and fell backwards onto the cage floor. I slammed the door shut and stood there looking at him. I breathed a sigh of relief and locked the cage. Quickly I walked to the end cage and shot the lock. Dan crawled to his feet and slowly pushed the door open. I nodded to the cage next to him; he stumbled into it to pick up the girl lying on the floor. She groaned as he slipped his arms under her and lifted her off the ground. At least she was still alive.

I bent to help Megan up. She put an arm around my shoulders then we headed for the door.

"Emery, you asshole! What the fuck are you doing? She's mine!" Jakob was screaming in panic now. All self-control lost.

I ignored him, slowly the four of us walked to the top of the stairwell and out into the morning sun. I could still hear his desperate screams as I put Megan down on the ground. I turned to look down the stairwell. I gave the pistol to her and cast a glance at the van.

"Emery, what are you doing?" Megan asked in alarm. Dan said nothing. "Justice," I replied as I climbed in to the driver's seat.

Slowly I backed the van up, aiming the exhaust towards the stairwell. The van dropped in to the hole with the rear tire spinning uselessly. The gas gauge read three-quarters of a tank.

"More than enough," I thought as I climbed out. Gently I picked Megan off the ground. I looked at Dan, and slowly we walked across the field leaving Jakob behind, with the van still running.

Chapter 50

Megan stood in front of me. Her ankle was reconstructed. Jakob had broken it to the extent that she needed to have pins put through the bones, and it was almost now fully fused together. She had limited movement in it, but at least she could walk again.

"Did you read the papers?" she asked as she moved gingerly around the hospital room. I had but didn't answer.

"They found him. He was locked in a cage, underground. They had to remove the van and send in people with breathing gear to recover his body." She was looking sideways at me.

"Shame," I replied, looking at the linoleum floor. I was beginning to hate the smell of hospitals. Nothing good could be found here, only sickness and death.

"You shouldn't have left him there like that, Emery," she stated. I shrugged my shoulders and looked at her.

"As far as I'm concerned, he got what he deserved," I replied. Megan looked away.

"I'm going home. I don't want to be here anymore," she said quietly. I looked at her and knew that she wasn't going to be persuaded otherwise.

I nodded and walked for the door.

THE END

Author's Biography

I'm 43 and Live in rural Waikato, New Zealand. I worked for Air New Zealand, the National carrier as an aircraft engineer for 12 years and went on to complete my pilots licence.

My hobbies include the outdoors and flying and of course writing.

This is my first completed novel featuring Emery. I have a second that is completed and a third underconstruction.

I took up writing as a challenge and have found that I can't pull myself away from it. I'm always looking for ideas to use and things to add which I hope would make the story more interesting for the reader.